AND THE CURIOUS CHRISTMAS TRUCK

L.M. WILLIAMS

Nicki Noel and the Curious Christmas Truck

ISBN-13: 978-1541022447
ISBN-10: 1541022440

DEDICATION

For our son, The Boy. You can do anything and be anything you want. Never let anyone tell you that you can't. Mommy and Dah-ee love you very much, and always will, simply because you're you.

Prologue

"I FEAR CHRISTMAS is in serious danger."

The room was dark, almost completely black except for a wobbly light that loomed above an older man. He stood in the middle of the room and the bright lamp overhead made it seem like he was being interrogated at a police station, or standing beneath a spotlight on a stage.

Six chairs formed a semi-circle in front of him. They all remained hidden in the shadows, sitting just outside of the bright circle that slowly swept back and forth across the floor. A faint outline of tiny bodies could barely be seen in each chair, and pairs of legs dangled over the edges of the seats. The one who'd spoken leaned forward in the center chair and his pale face dipped into the light. Atop his head rested a fuzzy green hat, and ears sprouted from each side unlike those of humans, but instead, extended and grew to a point. His eyes appeared large and round, and his eyebrows pinched together. When he spoke, his teeth jutted out like sharp jagged fangs. Giftavius was one of the six elder elves who formed the Council of Christmas—the chairman, in fact.

The old man stepped back at the sight of Giftavius, and his eyes squinted. "I'm sorry." The old man stared down at his shoes and showed Giftavius the top of his wool stocking cap. "I'm trying, but it's difficult, after—"

"We understand what you have been through. It pains all of us." Giftavius held two palms out to the darkness surrounding them and shook his head. "But Christmas should not be the dark time that it has become."

Giftavius pointed at the air next to the old man. He snapped his fingers and two glowing snowflakes flickered and circled each other before taking on a life of their own with a loud whoosh. They zigged and zagged around the old man, darting here and there, then sped up and collided next to him. Upon ramming into each other, a shiny beam formed like a portal into another world.

"Look at the city. How it was, before—"

The old man stared at the light as if it were a television screen.

In the middle stood a magnificent Christmas tree. It towered more than 80 feet tall and lifted up between the skyscrapers. Crowds of people clothed in scarves and coats and Christmas sweaters stood around admiring its beauty. A thick blanket of gorgeous white snow enveloped the city. People talked in the streets, and all of them smiled and laughed. When the lights from the tree—a mix of red, white, green, and gold—illuminated the city, their mouths all dropped open at the sight. Carolers belted out familiar Christmas melodies and the children all smiled. Their round, youthful faces beamed at the tree with thoughts of Santa Claus flying into town with his sleigh and reindeer at night while they slept.

The parents would glance down at their children and then, at the same time, they'd all crane their necks up at the crystal star on top of the tree. It represented a glimpse of hope in the inky night sky.

The old man stared at the projection and the corners of his mouth curled into a smile. He turned back to Giftavius and the others. Giftavius no longer appeared older and menacing, but instead, he sparkled of youth like one of the children on the screen. His smooth, chubby face returned the old man's smile.

"And eight years later, this—" Giftavius slouched into the chair and disappeared back into the darkness. "I'm afraid *this* is what it has become."

The old man's lips mashed into a thin line—his happiness short-lived.

Giftavius snapped his fingers once more, and the screen flashed to the present. People marched their children past an empty area where the tree once stood every Christmas season. They gripped their elbows and hurried along, shivering, without so much as a smile or a nod to greet those around them.

The city was gray and dirty. Despair covered everything like a thin film, the happiness all stripped away in the absence of the Christmas tree. A few faded red bows and wreaths dotted a couple of doors and other decorations were tattered and old, like they'd been hung and forgotten. The city lacked its heart. What once breathed life into the bustling metropolis had transformed into a machine—emotionless parts moving with a singular purpose and no interaction.

The old man could no longer look at the screen. His face was weathered and wrinkled. Even the hairs of his beard were shriveled and gray. His body drooped as though filled with sadness, mirroring the sorrow in his heart.

"I know," the old man said, looking down once more at his dirty work boots. His voice cracked when he repeated the two words. "I know."

Giftavius dropped to his feet. His black shoes curled up at his toes. He couldn't have been more than three feet tall, but to the old man he seemed like a giant hovering above.

Giftavius walked slowly toward the old man, and the old man's eyes darted to meet him. The screen remained lit at his side. The old man's heart squeezed tight in his chest, and he thought about the events many years ago responsible for the current situation.

Giftavius held out a card sealed with a dark red wax. "You shouldn't be afraid." Giftavius's teeth were razor sharp again and his eyebrows lowered into a scowl. He held out the envelope to the old man. "You know what to do with this, if you are able."

The old man's fingers trembled, but he reached out and took it from him. "I-I do. Tell him I will do my best."

"It's all that any of us can do." Giftavius turned sharply back to his chair.

The old man could make out the other elves' heads nodding in agreement. He spun on the heel of his boot and hurried from the room.

Giftavius leaned back in his chair. "Worry fills me. I pray we receive a Christmas miracle this year or all might be lost."

CHAPTER ONE

THE MAN IN THE SANTA SUIT

HIGH IN THE clouds, many miles above the city, a lone snowflake drifted through the air. Sometimes it would rise and then fall, or a quick gust of wind would shift its path into a sharp veer. As it slowly worked its way down, back and forth across the sky, the cloud that it fell from became smaller and the city beneath grew larger.

The snowflake curved sharply around a shiny silver skyscraper that was at times tall enough to pierce the bottoms of the clouds. It approached the roof of another building before an updraft blasted it back toward the heavens.

It hung, momentarily suspended in the air, then spiraled down in a flittering frenzy. Horns blared and engines roared from the streets below. The snowflake fluttered in the wind, twirling and gliding until it finally came to rest on the bridge of Nicki Noel's nose. Nicki's eyes had followed its entire path down to her, but they closed right before it made contact. The fluffy snowflake melted into tiny streams that ran down each side of her nose and tickled her cheeks. She giggled and sniffed in a large breath of air.

"I love how snow smells."

"Come on, Nicki, we're running late." Nicki's mother, Amanda Noel, tugged on Nicki's hand.

With her sandy blonde hair and bright blue eyes, Nicki appeared the spitting-image of her mother. However, in all of her eight years, what she had in common with her father held her curiosity most. Nicholas Noel disappeared shortly after Nicki came into the world. She'd only ever known life with her mother. When Nicki asked about her father—and she asked about him a lot, in fact—many different answers met her, all of them unsatisfying.

"You're not old enough."

"You're too young to understand."

"You'll find out one day."

"Not now, Nicki. It's not the right time."

Nicki thought the responses were unfair. She deserved to know about her dad.

There weren't many questions that Nicki didn't ask—about anything. She wanted to know how and why everything in the world worked.

Her mother would usually try to stop and explain things to her. But sometimes she would answer with, *"Because it just does."* or *"Because I said so, okay?"* It never stopped Nicki from asking more questions though. She was a very curious little girl.

Nicki skipped next to her mother down the busy sidewalk. Clouds of steam billowed from vents in the concrete and then lingered in the air above them. Every minute or so the subway would roar past, and the ground would shake and vibrate beneath their feet. It was so loud they'd have to stop talking or they wouldn't be able to hear one another.

Nicki's eyes darted around the city in search of two things: Christmas decorations and trucks. Trucks meant everything to Nicki. However, she found out—on multiple occasions—they were an odd thing for a little girl to like. But Nicki didn't care.

Trucks had massive, powerful engines. They carried things that needed carried, and did things that needed done—things that were impossible for ordinary people. But those weren't the only reasons. There was something, down in the depths of Nicki, that just loved trucks. She couldn't explain what drew her to them but deep inside she just felt it.

"Where did you get that shirt?" Amanda looked down at Nicki and then back up to the other pedestrians.

"I found it in my closet. Can you believe that?"

Nicki smiled up at Amanda Noel's beautiful face. A face that appeared far too young for a single mother one year away from turning thirty.

Amanda glared at Nicki's ratty long-sleeved shirt with a big truck printed on the front.

Bam!

Nicki slammed into a fuzzy red leg and stumbled backwards.

"Ow!" The man hobbled before quickly righting himself. He muttered a few words with a thick New England accent.

"I'm sorry!" Nicki had been skipping—she skipped pretty much everywhere since she'd learned how—and ran into the man walking on the sidewalk.

"Nicki! I've told you more than once. You have to watch where you're going, Sweetie. Are you okay, Sir?"

Nicki's eyes roamed cautiously up to the man's face, and she rubbed them to make sure that she wasn't dreaming. She trembled with excitement in the happiest of ways, and her cheeks flushed with pink hues. It was the man dressed as Santa Claus who always stood in front of the shop around the corner during Christmas time. He collected money from people and used it to buy gifts for children whose families couldn't afford toys for Christmas. He'd also buy them food so they could fill their bellies full with a nice Christmas dinner. Any money Nicki came across in winter, even pennies she found on the ground, *always* made it into his bucket.

Nicki knew he wasn't the real Santa Claus, but she'd heard from reliable sources that he worked directly for the big guy, Santa himself, at the North Pole.

How could he not work for Santa Claus?

Look at all the wonderful things he does, Nicki had thought to herself.

"I'm fine. Kids will be kids." Santa's fake white beard bobbed up and down when he spoke. He raised a fist to his mouth and coughed. A cloud of steam poofed around his hand in the chilly air.

"What's wrong?" Nicki asked.

"Whadda ya mean, Kid?" asked the man.

"You're always so happy, but today you look sad."

Nicki had noticed that Santa's cheeks weren't as rosy, and he didn't laugh heartily like he usually did.

"Nicki, it's not polite to tell people they look sad." Amanda stared at her daughter like she was a funny-looking bug.

"It's okay, it's just—" The man sighed. "They said I can't work in front of the store this year. Who'd have thought? You try and do something nice in this city and somebody always has to complain, yanno?" He shook his head at Amanda.

Amanda looked as if she felt bad for the man, but she began to tap her foot on the ground. She and Nicki were already late. "That's awful. Come on, Nicki. We're running late." Her mother pulled on Nicki's hand.

It wasn't enough of an explanation for Nicki Noel though. "What? Why? Who will ring the bell? Who will feed the children? Who will take toys? Who will I give my money to?"

The man chuckled and glanced to Amanda. "Wow, she sure can ask some questions, can't she?"

Amanda's eyes widened and her eyebrows rose almost to her hairline. "Ohhh, yes."

Nicki stood with her arms folded across her thin chest and scowled.

"Look, Kid. I'm sorry—okay? Some people just don't like Christmas. It's not like it used to be." He nodded over to a vacant area in front of one of the largest buildings in the city.

The place where giant, magnificent, wondrous Christmas trees once stood each year. Christmas trees full of lights, and garland, and tinsel, and ornaments—trees so stupendous that they inspired cheer and hope and kindness and gift-giving all over the city. Nicki wasn't old enough to remember, but she asked questions about them constantly.

"They told you to leave because they don't like Christmas?" Nicki pulled free from her mother's hand, forbidding it to hurry her along and end the conversation.

"I dunno, Kid. They just said I couldn't be there. Who knows? Corporate policy or somethin'. Some people think Christmas is offensive I guess, yanno? Religious stuff. I'm just Santa Claus. I ain't handing out Bibles or nothin'. But it is what it is. I'll think of somethin', okay?" It seemed as if he could sense Nicki's concern and wanted to set her at ease. "I'll find a place that'll let me ring my bell and take money. I promise."

"Okay." Nicki's eyes lit up and sparkled. All the sadness rushed out of her. "I'll bring you a dollar to your new place. I just got my allowance." Nicki flashed Santa a toothy grin though a few gaps appeared from teeth she'd lost.

He faced Amanda. "This is a fine girl you got here." Then he turned and patted Nicki on the head playfully. "Don't ever change, Kid."

"Thank you." Amanda nodded and dragged Nicki along. "Come on, Sweetie. You can't be late to school again."

Chapter Two

Girls Can't Drive Trucks

AMANDA KISSED NICKI on the forehead out in front of the school. "See you when you get home. Okay, Sweetie?"

"Okay."

"I can't believe you wore this raggedy shirt and I didn't even notice. I'm so failing you." Amanda smiled and jokingly shook her head at the truck on Nicki's shirt.

"I love this shirt. And you're doing just fine. I'm happy, see?" Nicki grinned as big as she could and rubbed her nose back and forth on her mom's. It was something they always did—a tradition. They called them Eskimo kisses.

"You're too smart for your own good, you

know? Now get to class. I love you."

"I love you too, Mommy."

Nicki skipped across the lawn and up the steps. She turned and waved goodbye to her mother. Amanda stood and watched until Nicki disappeared into the building.

Nicki's shoes squeaked on the shiny white tiles in the hallway. She walked as fast as she could to class. Running wasn't allowed. Nicki—and most of the other students—were often reminded of this fact by the teachers. Most kids loved to run and Nicki couldn't understand why it was frowned upon. The squeaky hallway was the perfect place for running.

Her teacher smiled when she skipped through the doorway to the classroom. "You made it. Just in time."

Nicki headed to her desk and opened the drawer.

A couple of boys snickered behind her while she rifled through markers and a stack of paper they used to draw pictures on or make up stories. Nicki spun around and glared. "What's funny?"

"Your shirt." The boys continued to laugh.

Nicki gritted her teeth. "What's funny about it?"

"It has a truck on it," the other boy said as if Nicki should catch on.

"So?" Nicki shrugged.

One of them stared at her like she was a strange alien. "Girls can't drive trucks."

Heat rushed into Nicki's face. "Says who?" She squeezed her fingers around the cold metal frame of her chair.

"Says everyone. Don't you know anything? Look around." The boy turned his head to the other girls in the class.

They all wore dresses with flowers on them or shirts with pictures of Powerpuff Girls and other girly cartoons that Nicki didn't care about.

"I'll drive a truck someday." Nicki lifted her head and puffed out her chest.

The boys burst into laughter and the teacher frowned at the ruckus. They both held a hand over their mouths and continued chuckling.

"You? Drive a truck? You probably think Santa Claus is real too."

Nicki's whole body tensed and she stared lasers at the two boys.

They both sat up straight at their desks.

"Santa Claus *is* real!"

The boys shook their heads and one of them said, "Nuh uh."

Nicki couldn't believe the boys would think Santa Claus wasn't real. How could they be so dumb? How else did the toys get under the tree at Christmas? Why would Christmas even exist if there was no Santa? But more than that, every December Nicki would feel butterflies in her stomach. Something deep down inside of her knew that Christmas was special and that Santa Claus was, in fact, very very real.

✻ ✻ ✻

Nicki took the bus home from school even though her Mom had dropped her off that morning. It was their routine every weekday. Amanda would go to work at the office and Nicki would ride the bus home. They almost always arrived at the house around the same time.

Nicki hopped off the bus and skipped inside, but she was a little less bouncy than usual. It was Friday and that meant a whole weekend of her and her mom decorating the house. But Nicki didn't have her usual pep. When she finally made it to the door her feet dragged against the ground.

The boys at school had gotten to her. She'd began to doubt if girls could ever drive trucks. Trucks and Christmas were all Nicki ever thought about, even in July. She knew everything there was to know about both of them. But the more she'd thought about it, she realized she'd never met a girl who drove a truck.

What if the boys were right about the trucks?

Nicki hung her head and pushed through the front door.

"Nicki, is that you?"

She immediately took off toward her mother's voice. "Mom, boys at school say girls can't drive trucks. And—" She walked into the kitchen and Amanda paced back and forth with the phone to her ear. She held a finger up to let Nicki know to be quiet.

"Yeah, I understand. I can't take her with me. Are you sure she can't stay with you a few days? It's for work or I wouldn't ask. Okay, okay. No, it's okay. I'll ask Madeline. Thanks, bye."

Amanda hung up the phone and exhaled a long breath. She plopped down on a barstool and leaned her back against the kitchen counter.

Nicki stared at Amanda.

Amanda stared back. "What is it?"

Nicki looked up at Amanda's eyes, the stress apparent on her face loud and clear. Nicki had heard grownups talk about stress before and understood the look. Amanda's hair was pulled up into a messy bun and she slumped on the bar stool. For most people, maybe that was normal, but Amanda had great posture and constantly told Nicki to stop slouching and to sit up straight.

"The boys at school." Nicki slowed down and took a breath. "They told me girls can't drive trucks and that Santa isn't real." Nicki marched past her mother. Her anger revived along with her energy. "Can you believe they said that?" She climbed on top of a stool in front of the cabinets and reached for a glass. Once in her grasp, she walked towards the refrigerator and pulled out a half-gallon of milk. "Santa Claus isn't real? They *actually* said that. Stupid boys." She shook her head in disbelief.

Amanda, apparently not thinking, muttered, "Finally, the truth."

Nicki stood, shell shocked. She'd pulled the cap off the milk and the carton slipped right through her fingers. It landed upright on the floor, but white liquid exploded through the top like a geyser and splattered onto the tile.

"Nicki, be careful!" Amanda hadn't looked at Nicki as she stood up to get a towel.

When she glanced down Nicki had tears in the corners of her eyes and her bottom lip quivered. Nicki glared up at Amanda.

"Oh, Honey. No. I'm sorry. Of course Santa Claus is real. And of course girls can drive trucks. Those boys were just being silly."

Nicki shook her head and a single tear trickled down her cheek and dripped onto the truck shirt. "Y-you used y-your serious v-voice."

Amanda took Nicki into her arms and squeezed her tight. "I'm sorry. I didn't mean—"

Nicki shook under Amanda's touch. "I-I don't care what you or those b-boys say. I know h-he's real." Nicki wanted to run to her room and slam the door. She knew what she knew, but something about her mother's arms always made her sadness go away faster. It was her safe place.

"Sweetie, I'm sorry. I had a rough day, okay?" Amanda leaned back and put her palms on Nicki's cheeks. "And I'm sorry about this weekend, but I have to go out of town for work. It's why I was on the phone."

Nicki's brain often raced and her thoughts would jumble together. She'd already moved on and her tears had started to dry on her cheeks. Then her mother hit her with this news too. "But—but you said we could decorate for Christmas."

"I know. And I'm really sorry. They won't let me take you. You're going to have to stay with someone."

"This isn't fair!" Nicki stomped on the ground,

one foot after the other. She'd been looking forward to this weekend for months.

"I'll make it up to you. I promise. Please don't make this harder on me, Nicki. I'm sad about it too."

Nicki started to calm, and she realized it wasn't her mother's fault. Her mom always got as excited as she did about decorating the house together. "It's okay, Mom." Nicki rubbed the back of Amanda's arm. "So where am I going?"

Amanda sighed. "I don't know yet. Your Grandma has something going on, so I need to call your Aunt Madeline and see if you can stay with her."

Nicki's face heated up, but she tried her best to hide her irritation. "I don't want to stay with her. I want to stay with Grandma! Aunt Madeline's house smells like spider breath."

Amanda giggled. "Spider breath? Really?"

"Well it smells like something over there." Nicki shook her head and tried to look serious.

They both burst into a fit of laughter.

Amanda wrapped an arm around Nicki. "Go play in your room for a bit. I'll let you know as soon as I hear something. Get a bag ready because we have to leave tonight, okay?"

"Fine. But you owe me. We're baking extra batches of cookies *and* I want a truck ornament for the tree. An 18-wheeler. Not a pick-up." Nicki folded her arms across her chest and grinned.

"Okay. Fine. I promise. And I mean it."

Nicki headed toward her room, but she

stopped just far enough down the hall that Amanda couldn't see her in the shadows.

Amanda made two more phone calls. Aunt Madeline had some kind of antique collectible show, so she was out. Nicki pumped her fist. One of Amanda's close cousins couldn't watch her either and Nicki sat down with her back against the wall. She didn't want to stay at her Aunt Madeline's, but she started to think that everyone in the world was too busy for her. She pulled her knees to her chest and leaned down so that her head rested on top of them while she stared down at the floor.

Amanda muttered, "What am I going to do? Ugh!"

Nicki crawled around and peeked into the kitchen where Amanda paced back and forth once more, talking to herself. "I can't call them. It's been too long. They probably haven't forgiven Nicholas and I for running away. They don't even know about her."

Nicki giggled into her palm. She always found it funny when her mother talked to herself, which she did often, even in her sleep sometimes.

Amanda stood and inspected the phone. To Nicki it seemed like hours even though it was probably only a few seconds. Amanda finally pressed the button and held the phone to her ear. "Hello, Grant? Is Elizabeth there? It's Amanda." A few seconds passed and Nicki heard a loud squeal come through the phone. Amanda jolted upright and held the phone away from her ear until it stopped. "Yeah, it's me. I promise. I know. I know. Yeah. I'm sorry it's been so long. Uh huh, yeah." Amanda nodded. "It'd be great to catch up with you too. Listen, here's the thing—" Amanda's eyes rolled up to the ceiling then back down. She sighed. "Nicholas and I have a daughter."

More squealing.

Loud squealing.

Nicki grinned and wanted to laugh.

The thought of someone getting that excited about anything made her happy.

Who was this Elizabeth? Nicki thought to herself.

"I have to leave on business. It's an emergency or I wouldn't ask. I need someone to watch Nicki for two or three days, tops."

Amanda had worked so hard after Nick was gone. She'd raised Nicki virtually on her own for eight years. But somehow, she'd managed to only take a year off and still graduate college at twenty-three. She'd finally reunited with her family once she had things together— a good job, stable home life—but she always remained secretive about Nick's family and friends. As far as Nicki knew she'd only met them once or twice, and it was before her parents had ran away together.

"Really? You can? You're a life saver! I promise you she's well-behaved. Barely makes any messes."

More squealing.

Elizabeth was definitely a squealer. Nicki found herself wondering how Grant handled all the squeals.

"You're still in the same house on the mountain? Awesome. I'll bring her by tonight. She'll have everything she needs. Can't wait to see you too. Bye."

Nicki quickly realized she was supposed to be in her room. She bounded down the hall and through the doorway. She spun two full circles trying to figure out how to make it look like she'd been there the whole time her mom was on the phone. Her room was neat and tidy, the toys all in their designated spots. Nicki assigned places where all her toys belonged and she never left them out or it would drive her crazy.

Her head whirled dizzily from all the spinning and she stumbled in a zig-zag pattern to one of her toy chests. She pried it open and pulled out a couple toy trucks and sat down in the floor with them. One was a big diesel Mack truck with a trailer attached, and the other a fueler truck with a large metal tank on the rear.

Amanda opened the door and Nicki looked up pretending to be surprised.

"Oh, umm, hi, Mom. I'm just playing with my trucks here, just like I've been doing the whole time since you told me to."

Amanda crossed her arms and stared with a smile that suggested she knew exactly what Nicki was up to.

Nicki wondered how her mom could always tell when she was making something up. She *always* knew!

"I'm not even going to worry about what you were doing, because I found someone you can stay with. Come sit on the bed, Sweetie."

Amanda walked over and plopped down on Nicki's bed. She patted one of the trucks sewn into the comforter.

"Who is it?" Nicki skipped over and took a seat where her mother's hand had been.

"Two friends, from a long time ago." Amanda smiled at Nicki's huge, bright blue eyes. "They were friends of your father's."

A huge wave of joy coursed through Nikki's chest and then seemed to explode like fireworks inside of her. Her heart thumped against her rib cage like a dog's tail wagging against a wall.

Thump-thump-thump.

"Really?"

Amanda nodded. "Really. And I need you to behave for them, okay? Can you do that for me, please? And when I get back, we will do all the Christmas things we usually do."

"I will be better than good. I will be the bestest ever."

"Good. I figured you might be a little excited."

Both of them fell back onto the bed, their heads next to one another, staring up at the ceiling.

"I'm sorry I haven't told you more about him, Sweetie. It's just hard sometimes, figuring out what you're old enough to know and not know."

"It's okay to tell me, Mommy. I'm bigger than you think."

Amanda's eyes rolled over to her daughter. Eight years had gone by so fast. "I know you are. We're just figuring this stuff out together. It's just you and me, you know? We're a team."

"I love our team," Nicki said.

"I do too." Amanda lightly pinched Nicki's nose and wiggled it.

"Unless you tell me Santa Claus isn't real."

Amanda chuckled. "Christmas is a tough time of the year for me, Nicki. I try to be happy because I love it so much. But I lost a huge chunk of my life around the holidays, and I just get sad sometimes, okay? But I try my best, for you. I just wish you could've seen the city when the tree would go up. Everything was so different then."

"I know. I've looked at all the pictures. Now nobody but me really cares."

"I know. It's so sad." Amanda's face brightened. "You should've seen it though. The truck that would haul the tree through town. You'd have talked about it for days. It was huge and bright red and the trailer seemed to stretch for miles."

"Whoa? Hold on. You're telling me that there was a giant truck to go along with the huge Christmas tree?" Nicki's long dark eyelashes fluttered.

Amanda laughed. "Oh yes. It was a good time. It really was." Amanda's smile turned to a frown as she stared at her daughter.

"What is it, Mom?"

Amanda shook her head, as if clearing her mind from whatever thought had caused her sadness. "It's nothing. Just pack your bag and let's get going, okay?" She tried to fake a smile for Nicki then turned her gaze to the wall.

"You can tell me. I want to know."

Amanda turned back. "I just see your dad sometimes when I look at you. That's all. I miss him so much."

Nicki wrapped her arms around her mom and nuzzled her head against her shoulder. "It's okay. We're a team. Maybe Christmas will make you happy again one day, the way it makes me happy."

Amanda rubbed her hand back and forth on Nicki's arm. "Maybe, Sweetie. Maybe."

Chapter Three

The House on the Mountain

THE CAR CURVED up a long driveway to a little cottage-style house perched on a flat area. Elizabeth and Grant lived on one of the foothills that sat in front of really large mountains with snowy peaks that looked like jagged rocks in the distance. Still, the mountain they lived on was tall enough that Nicki could look down at the city from the house.

Amanda and Nicki got out and Amanda fiddled with the trunk when...

Squealing.

More squealing.

Elizabeth flew out of the house with open arms and smothered Nicki in a hug. Grant walked around and gave Amanda a normal, less-excited squeeze.

"Oh my gosh! Look at you! You look just—" Elizabeth froze for a quick second and glanced over to Amanda. She whipped back to a smiling Nicki and squished her cheeks on each side. "I'm so happy you came to stay with us."

More squealing.

Nicki didn't usually like people squishing her cheeks, but this time she didn't mind so much. She grinned sheepishly at Elizabeth, but then her eyes darted up the side of the mountain to another house way off in the distance. Her mouth fell open and she gasped when she saw the huge, bright red truck that sat out front.

It was *the* truck!

The one her mother described!

The one Nicki had noticed in all the pictures when she went back through them!

Her heart sped up like a race car engine.

The truck, the one that once carried the Christmas tree into town. She would've recognized it from anywhere.

Elizabeth wrapped Nicki in a hug for the zillionth time, zapping all the air out of her making it hard for her to breathe. She forgot about the truck for a moment while she gave her best effort to return Elizabeth's welcoming hug. Then she walked around the car, glancing to the truck and then back to her mother.

Nicki's chest began to ache a little and her legs grew heavy. She saw tears in the corners of her mother's eyes. It always happened when she was about to go away for a little while and leave her with someone. Nicki's stomach started to roll and twist at the thought of spending the night in a new home, with people she didn't yet know, in a bed she'd never slept in, even if the Christmas tree truck was where she could see it.

She finally made it over to her mom and hugged her tightly. Amanda ran her fingers through Nicki's hair.

"It'll be over before you know it. Then it'll be time for Christmas, okay?"

Nicki sniffled and thought about falling asleep without her mom in the room next to her. "Please don't go, Mommy."

"Hey." Amanda lifted Nicki's chin with one finger so that she could see her eyes. "Remember how big and brave you said you were? Back at the house? How you can handle things?"

Nicki's bottom lip trembled, but she managed to nod. "Yeah," she squeaked out.

"I need you to be big and brave for me, okay?"

"You'll call?"

"Of course I'll call, Sweetie."

Elizabeth leaned back into Grant's arms with a big, warm smile.

"Video call?" Nicki asked.

Amanda glanced over to Elizabeth.

"We've got Skype on the computer, and Grant just got one of those smart phones. So it shouldn't be a problem."

"You hear that? We can video call as soon as I get there."

"O-okay."

Amanda wiped a tear from Nicki's eye. "I'll miss you so so much. But I'll be back soon. I promise."

Nicki nodded hesitantly at her mother. "I love you."

"Ohh, I love you too, Sweetie. Come here."

And after one last hug, Amanda climbed into the car and waved before disappearing down the mountain road.

❄ ❄ ❄

A few hours passed, and Nicki had all but forgotten her mom had even left. Grant and Liz (as she'd told Nicki to call her) were two of the happiest people she'd ever met. They laughed and joked and Nicki loved it at their house almost immediately.

Nicki pulled out her bag of toys she'd brought and scattered a few trucks around on the carpet. She lined them up on an imaginary road and then hooked up trailers to each one.

"Like trucks, do ya?" Grant raised an eyebrow.

It was like a light bulb went off in Nicki's brain, and she remembered the Christmas tree truck she'd spotted earlier. "Yes, Sir. Very much."

"Please, don't call me Sir. Grant is fine."

"Sorry." Nicki hung her head like she was in trouble.

"Oh, no. It's okay. Don't be sad. I'm just saying, you can call me Grant. But if you want to say Sir, feel free."

Nicki smiled. "Hey, umm, Sir? I mean, umm, Grant?"

Grant chuckled. "Yeah? What's up?"

"I saw a truck up the hill. I recognized it from old Christmas pictures. It's the one that used to haul the tree, isn't it?"

Grant's eyes darted over to Liz who shrugged

like she didn't know what to say.

Grant looked back at Nicki. "You know, I think you're right."

Before she could contain herself, Nicki's happiness overwhelmed her. And, as usual, it came out of her mouth in the form of a bunch of rapid-fire questions. "Who lives there? What happened to the truck? Does it still run? How long do you think it is? It has to be a hundred feet long, right? What's it doing up there?"

Grant's mouth fell open in surprise.

Nicki took notice and turned her gaze back to the floor again. "Sorry, I get super excited about trucks and Christmas."

Grant kept staring back and forth between her and Liz. Nicki wondered how he didn't get dizzy with his eyes moving so fast.

"Look, umm, Nicki. The thing is—" He squeezed his eyes almost all the way shut, like he was trying to think of what to say. "I know you're excited about that truck. It's a very neat truck. *But*, you need to stay away from that house, okay?"

"Why?" Nicki gave Grant an inquisitive look.

"Well, I mean, it's a ways away. And it's through the woods. There are wild animals. And the man who lives there—"

Liz walked over and sat down on the floor next to Nicki.

Grant continued once Liz had an arm around her. "The man who lives there is kind of mean. And he has a big dog that doesn't like children much. He doesn't want visitors and he lives all alone with the dog and the truck."

"Oh." Nicki looked down at her trucks and scooted them around on the carpet. "Okay."

"I'm very sorry, Nicki."

"Hey." Liz perked up and put her palms on Nicki's cheeks. "How about some hot chocolate? Your mom should be calling in a little bit anyway, and then it'll be time for bed."

"Do you put marshmallows in it?"

Liz bugged her eyes out at Nicki. "Is there any other way to drink hot chocolate? Of course we put marshmallows in it!"

Nicki grinned. "Mmm, yes please."

Liz stood up and started toward the kitchen.

Nicki glanced around the living room. It was so cozy and friendly there, but only pictures of Grant and Elizabeth hung on the walls. Something was missing, like dogs or kids. *It's a great house for dogs or children*, Nicki thought.

"Why don't you guys have any kids?"

Liz stopped walking for a second, but didn't turn around.

"You'd be great parents. You make me happy and I've only been here a couple hours."

Grant leaned forward in his chair. Liz still had her back to them.

"That's a very nice thing for you to say, Nicki. Very very nice. Liz and I would love to have children, but unfortunately, we can't."

"Oh." Nicki felt awful, like she'd said something she shouldn't have. She felt that way a lot. She often said things without thinking first. "I'm sorry you can't have any kids. I wish you could. I love it here."

She noticed a hand go up to Liz's face, though Liz continued to look away. Nicki cringed when she thought she'd made Liz sad.

"C-can I come back? Again sometime? After my mom comes to get me? Your house is way better than the other places I usually stay."

Liz turned around and sped over to Nicki. She sat down on the floor and smiled a big smile. Her eyes were pink and puffy like she wanted to cry. Liz wrapped her arms around Nicki and pulled her in close so she could kiss the top of her head. "Of course you can. You can come here whenever you want, any time you want. You are *always* welcome here."

Nicki managed to sneak a glance at Grant who smiled from the recliner. He rocked back and forth, and gave Nicki a thumbs up. She giggled and flashed him one back. Nicki couldn't remember a time that she was happier than this when her mother was away.

"So, in the morning—how about we have breakfast and then you can go outside and play in the yard? Get some fresh air? That sound like a plan?" Grant asked.

"Yep," Nicki said.

"But right now, hot chocolate. Then your video call with your mom. I think she's going to want to see your pretty face." Liz stood and then walked back to the kitchen.

"Hot chocolate before bed? Sounds like a plan to me," Nicki said.

Laughter from the three of them escaped the cozy little house on the mountainside and faded into the night.

Chapter Four

The Old Man and His Dog

Nicki Noel wolfed down her breakfast the next morning—a Saturday. Usually she watched cartoons and played with her trucks in front of the television while at home in the city. She and Amanda often ate breakfast together on the floor, or the couch. Then they might run errands, go shopping, or walk the sidewalk at the park and stare out at the mountains.

None of this, however, was the reason Nicki ate her food as fast as she possibly could. Nicki wanted to play outside. More than that, she wanted to get a better look at the Christmas tree truck.

Grant loved bacon and it seemed like Elizabeth liked to cook it, because the whole house smelled just like, well, bacon. Nicki didn't object. Liz also cooked scrambled eggs and toast with butter and grape jelly. Nicki shoveled the last forkful of eggs into her mouth, washing it all down with a cold glass of milk.

She looked up and Grant stared at her over the top of his newspaper. He cocked an eyebrow up and asked, "Hungry?"

Nicki giggled. "Just excited to play outside."

Elizabeth took her plate and carried it to the sink.

"I can wash my plate if you want? I know how."

"Nonsense," Elizabeth said. "You're our guest."

Nicki felt like she could get used to this place. At her house, she *had* to wash her own plate.

Grant motioned toward the back door with his head. "Go on." He smiled.

"Are you sure? I can help out—"

"You need to go burn off all that food you just inhaled."

Nicki smiled again. She'd smiled more at the Merriwether's house than she could remember smiling anywhere else. "Thank you, Sir. I mean, umm, Grant."

Grant chuckled and went back to his paper.

As Nicki headed toward the back door with her bag of toys, Grant said, "Don't go past the trees, okay?"

"I won't. I promise."

❄ ❄ ❄

Nikki sat on the ground near a fresh pile of

dirt she'd found. No matter how hard she tried to concentrate on her toys, she couldn't help but stare up at the Christmas tree truck. She glanced back at the small house that she'd stayed in the night before. Her eyes roamed the white exterior and red brick chimney. Nicki found the yellow shutters that framed each window an odd color choice, but she thought Liz a bit quirky and shrugged it off.

Nicki looked around at the mountains and trees surrounding her. Many of the trees sat naked, having lost all their leaves back in the fall, but some, like the evergreens, stuck out the same as Nicki did when she played in a room full of girls. She turned her gaze to the much larger house near the Christmas tree truck. She took in the slate gray exterior, her eyes drifting to the black shutters. She imagined it creaking and groaning and making all sorts of noises at night.

Nicki turned back to the line of trees Grant warned her not to go past. The towering timber only lay about fifty feet away. Nicki, an explorer at heart, loved pretending she was going on adventures back home when she played in her backyard. But she liked the Merriwether's very much and didn't want to get into any kind of trouble by following her imagination on some crazy journey.

I'll just play with my trucks. I have all this dirt. This will be fun.

She'd brought every kind of truck and machinery she could think of—dump trucks, mixer trucks, semi-trucks, gassers, fire trucks, and pick-ups, along with scoops, tractors, combines, dozers, backhoes, trailers, Bobcats, and scrapers—and what she had was perfect for her new play area. Nicki grabbed a dump truck for dumping and a backhoe for scooping. She loaded the dirt into the dump truck with the backhoe, scoop by scoop, and then she would wheel the dump truck to the other side and unload it. Load by load she created a pile of dirt on one side, and pretended she was clearing a path for a new road being built. Then she used her scraper to smooth the dirt for the new road.

The whole time she played she couldn't help but look up occasionally at the Christmas tree truck, and all sorts of questions popped into her mind.

Why doesn't it get the trees anymore? What's wrong with it? Is it broken? Who lives in the house and drives the truck? Who cuts down the tree? What kind of tools do they use?

A breeze kicked up in the tops of the trees. The branches rattled against one another. It started up by the Christmas truck and whooshed down the mountain toward Nicki. The trees all swayed back and forth like a wave heading right for her.

When it arrived, the wind kicked up and swirled. It scattered some of the loose dirt that she'd dumped into a pile and her hair whipped across her face. She pushed it back behind her ear. Nicki went to scoop the scattered dirt and move it back into the pile when she heard a voice that seemed to come from the wind as it twirled in every direction. The voice fell upon her like a whisper.

"Believe."

Her face paled and she thought she was imagining things at first. Nicki shook her head and went back to the dirt, pretending she'd imagined the words, not heard them loud and clear. But the wind kept whistling in her ears and blowing her hair back across her face.

"Save Christmas."

Nicki whipped her head around, as if she were trying to see the invisible voice. "Who is that? Who's talking?" She stared up at the Christmas truck.

Nicki wasn't sure what she felt, but it tugged on her like a force field, drawing her to the truck. She'd felt it ever since she'd arrived. But whose voice was talking to her? It couldn't be the truck.

Trucks can't talk, Nicki thought.

She told herself that she shouldn't go near it. Grant said the man and dog that lived there disliked children, and the woods were dangerous.

She didn't want to upset the Merriwethers, and she'd promised her mother that she'd behave and stay out of trouble. Nicki didn't like upsetting people, and she didn't like to disobey. Her stomach hurt just thinking about it.

Still, something about the truck tugged like a magnet, pulling on her. It grew stronger and stronger by the second. Nicki's curiosity was too much for her to bear.

Before she realized it, she stood tall in front

of the trees Mr. Merriwether warned about. She looked back at the house and then back to the leafless branches.

"Help me, Nicki," the wind murmured to her once more.

Without thinking, Nicki stepped into the trees and left all of her toys back with the dirt. She moved in the direction of the truck as if she'd traveled through the thick forest a thousand times. Her feet—with a mind of their own—knew the exact path to follow.

About ten minutes later, the trees cleared. She rubbed her eyes and stared with her mouth wide open.

There it was.

Right out in front of her.

The bright red truck.

Nicki smiled and her eyes widened as far as possible. "Whoa!"

It was the most beautiful truck she'd ever seen, and the trailer hooked to it seemed to stretch for miles into the distance behind it. It had two large silver pipes that sprouted up from the hood. *It looks like a diesel truck, and those must be the exhaust pipes*, she thought. She walked alongside the truck, her fingers brushing up against the cold metal. Nicki still wore the same truck shirt from yesterday and a pair of faded blue jeans which bunched up around the top of her sneakers.

She walked around to the driver's side door. Nicki stared up at the chrome handle that seemed a hundred feet high, impossible for her to ever reach. When she glanced over, the house appeared empty with no sign of a dog.

A matching chrome bar ran underneath the door and she stepped up onto it—determined. When Nicki found a challenge she rarely backed down. She tilted her head back to better assess her progress. Her target grew closer, but she feared it was still out of reach.

"Well, it's an improvement."

She reached up blindly as high as she could, straining her arm, but still fell short of the shiny chrome handle by several feet.

Nicki took in a deep breath and turned to her right.

A small foot rest jutted out higher on the side of the truck. She stepped onto it and stretched with everything she could possibly muster—groaning audibly in the process—until the ends of her fingers reached the metal. Nicki grunted and lifted high on the tips of her toes which ached from the weight of her body pressing down on them.

"Almost there. Sooo close."

Her fingers stung, pressing against the frigid steel handle, and her face appeared bright pink from her efforts coupled with the effects of a biting chill wind.

"Come onnn."

It refused to budge and Nicki feared it to be locked—her efforts meaningless. She also became keenly aware of how high she'd climbed and a shiver of fright crept up her spine.

Don't look down, Nicki. Do. Not. Look. Down.

Nicki looked down.

Her breath hitched and blood rushed from her face, leaving behind a pale expression of horror. Only a mere three feet separated her from the ground, but in Nicki's mind she teetered on the edge of a cliff, the tiny blades of grass thousands of feet below.

Through her worried state, she jammed her fingers into the handle with all of her strength.

Clack-wrshhhh!

The door whipped open. Nicki flailed and pawed for something to latch onto.

Kuh-dink kuh-donk kuh kuh.

The door swayed back and forth before coming to rest.

Nicki wobbled for a quick second that seemed far longer, before her frantic fingers found the seat and she steadied herself. She stifled a scream, her chest rising and falling rapidly as she huffed a few huge breaths.

Whew!

Nicki climbed up into the driver's seat. She could barely see over the steering wheel. Never in her life had she been inside of a big truck, let alone her favorite truck in the whole world: the Christmas tree truck.

"Let's do this, Truck!" She reached out for the wheel and pretended to steer and honk the horn dreaming of driving the big rig down the mountain with a tree strapped to the back. "Christmas will be saved this year!" She pretend-honked the loud horn again and imagined the faces of all the children lighting up at the sight of the tree.

Nicki looked down and noticed a pair of keys dangling from the ignition. She knew she shouldn't touch them, but she'd never wanted anything more than to hear the giant, powerful engine come to life. Slowly, her hand drifted toward the keys.

"What are you doing in there?" hollered a deep, scruffy voice.

Nicki screamed and her back hammered into the seat. Her eyes slammed shut and she refused to look where the voice came from.

She panted furiously and it felt like the whole world was closing in on her.

A vicious dog bark roared behind the man and drifted through all of the trees down the mountain. Nicki squeezed her eyes shut harder, wishing she hadn't disobeyed Mr. Merriwether. "I-I'm sorry." Tears squeezed between her eyelids and started to sting. She quickly blinked them away and kept her eyes shut.

"How'd you get here?" The voice was loud and insistent.

Nicki slowly lifted one eye open.

An old man. The one Grant warned about.

He stood there, scowling.

He had a silvery-white beard that covered half of his leathery face, and he wore overalls with a red and black flannel shirt under them. He was a large man—so large that he loomed above and cast a shadow over Nicki.

"Where'd you come from?" he shouted.

Nicki sobbed but couldn't manage any words. She pointed to the Merriwether's house.

The man whipped around and stared at Grant and Liz's place and then turned back. His mouth dropped open and all the color drained from his face. He stared Nicki up and down, a scowl returning.

"You're trespassing. And they don't have any kids. You're lying!"

Nicki sobbed. "I promise it's where I came from, Sir."

The old man sighed, and his voice softened a little at the sight of Nicki sobbing. "You can't come onto my property like this. And don't touch that key. This is a special truck. It's not some shiny toy."

"Y-yes, Sir."

The old man took a step back. He appeared to realize how harsh he'd been. He turned his mean stare to the ground. "All right, then. Hop on down from there."

Nicki's head swiveled toward the dog and she hesitated.

"He ain't gonna bite you."

She nodded and climbed down the truck. The dog walked over to sniff her and she winced.

"He's a guard dog and he don't like kids coming into his yard." The old man sneered.

The giant dog that looked like it was part wolf pressed his snout to her shirt and sniffed what seemed like a hundred times in a matter of seconds. Its nose tickled Nicki's ribs and she began to laugh. The dog licked her face. It tickled Nicki some more and she giggled, unable to stop herself.

"Traitor." The old man leered at the dog then turned to Nicki. "What's your name, anyway?"

"N-N-Nicki. Nicki Noel, Sir."

The old man shoved his hands in his pockets and continued to stare at Nicki like she was a puzzle he was trying to solve. "That's Brutus." He glared at Brutus, then took a step toward the house. "Follow me. We'll call them to come get you. Shouldn't be out walking through these woods alone. Coyotes and bears live out here. You gotta be more careful."

"Y-yes, Sir."

CHAPTER FIVE

HOT CHOCOLATE WITH THE OLD MAN

NICKI SAT DOWN on a chair at the old man's table while he walked over and picked up a telephone that looked at least twenty years old. Brutus lay down at Nicki's feet and stretched out his paws.

The house seemed like it had been very nice at one time, but now it was dusty and didn't appear well cared for. Dirty dishes piled on top of one another in the sink, and heaps of mail and all sorts of clutter strung around the counters and spilled onto the table. Nicki rocked back and forth a little just at the sight of it.

"You like hot chocolate?" The old man sneered.

Nicki began to think he didn't know how to smile.

"Yes. Do you have marshmallows?"

"No." He jammed a mug down on the counter.

Thwhack!

Nicki jolted upright in her chair.

The old man tossed some boxes around in a cabinet and pulled a packet from one of them. He dumped it into the mug and filled it with water. He stirred it no more than three times with a spoon he'd shoved into the cup. The old man dialed a number on the phone and slung the mug into the microwave.

He pressed a few buttons on the microwave and it whirred to life, heating Nicki's drink.

Beep beep beep.

Bzzzzz.

He scowled at Nicki, the phone held tightly against his ear.

"Elizabeth melted bars of chocolate into hers. She had marshmallows too."

"You want some or not?" The old man glared down his nose at Nicki.

She slumped in her chair. "Yes, please."

The man's cheeks dropped down and he sighed. "Sorry. My name is John. John Klaussen."

"Thank you for making me hot chocolate, Mister John Klaussen."

John's lips looked like they might just curl into a smile when Nicki heard a voice come through the phone. "Hello?"

"This some kind of joke you guys are playing down there? What's with the girl? Why's she up here on my property, messing with the truck? Didn't you tell her to stay away?"

He yanked the mug out when the microwave sounded, then walked over and dropped it on the table in front of Nicki. The hot liquid swished and sloshed, some of it spilling over the side. Steam rose up from it. It wasn't mixed all the way and there were tiny little chunks of cocoa powder bobbing up and down in the foam.

Nicki didn't care though. She blew on it and watched the steam wisp around in the air before disappearing. Somewhere deep inside of her she knew that John probably didn't make hot cocoa for just anyone that came over, and he was doing his best to be nice to her.

John kept staring over at Nicki and then he would cover the phone and whisper-scream where she couldn't hear.

His eyes grew wide and his teeth started to grind together. He stood up angrily and forgot to cover the phone and whisper. A vein popped out on his forehead.

"I don't have time! This has to be a joke."

John realized Nicki watched from the table and heard everything he was saying. He covered the phone back up with his palm and spoke through gritted teeth where Nicki couldn't hear. "My son would've told me. I don't care how mad he was when he ran away. He wouldn't hide this from me! And her name is wrong! All wrong! Does her mother even know she's here?" There was a pause and then he threw an arm in the air and rolled his eyes. "Fine! Fine! Whatever you say, Liz!"

He jammed the phone into the receiver, but it fell and clattered to the floor.

Eeeeep eep-eep-eep.

The droning sound emanated through the room as if even the phone was angry at not being hung up properly.

John backed away, staring at Nicki until his back rammed into the countertop. His face was pale as a ghost and his mouth agape. Nicki shrugged and blew on her hot chocolate again before taking a sip. The foam stuck to her upper lip and she licked it off. "Mmmm, this hot chocolate is really good. Thank you again, Sir."

John walked toward her slowly and scratched his silvery beard. He looked possessed, like he'd just seen Bigfoot or the Loch Ness Monster. Nicki chuckled a little.

"You okay, Mister John?"

He towered high above her. His shadow engulfed her tiny body as she sipped on her mug of cocoa.

John leaned down and put his palms on each of her cheeks then cocked his head sideways to examine her some more.

Nicki sat still, unsure what to do, but she didn't want to be rude. He still frightened her but not as much. Something in his expressions seemed to suggest that he was warming to her.

The corners of John's mouth curled up and his cheeks turned red and rosy. His eyes glossed over.

He smiled.

"Y-you have his eyes."

"Whose eyes?" Nicki mimicked him and cocked her head inquisitively to the side.

John shook his head. "Nothing. Nothing, don't worry about it." He stood back up but his eyes remained glued to Nicki. "I talked to Grant and Liz and they want you to stay the night here. They said we need *time* together," John scoffed.

A chill ran up Nicki's back, but somehow the truck outside gave her comfort. She didn't like staying at new places, and she really loved Liz and Grant's house.

The truck, or something, told you to come up here. Why would it do that unless the place was safe?

Nicki inhaled deeply through her nose. "It's gonna snow. I can tell these things. I can smell it."

John sniffed the air. "I think you just may be right, Kiddo."

Chapter Six

A Big Secret

NICKI SAT BY the roaring flames in the fireplace and kicked her feet up to rest them on the brick hearth. "I like my feet toasty." She wiggled her toes inside of her socks as they began heating up. "Whose eyes did you say I had, earlier?"

John seemed to be battling with himself and shook his head, muttering gibberish that Nicki didn't understand. He finally peered over to Nicki from the couch. "You need to know the truth, Kiddo. Come over here." He patted the cushion next to him.

Nicki walked over and took a seat. She missed the warmth of the fire already, but the cotton on her socks had heated enough that her toes remained toasty the way she liked.

When she sat down she sank into the soft seat cushion and stared up at John.

"My God, you look just like him." John's eyes glossed over like he might cry.

Nicki thought it strange for a man his size to cry about anything. But then she thought how the boys said a girl couldn't drive a truck. She knew they were wrong, and if a girl could drive a truck, why couldn't a big strong man like John cry if he wanted to?

"Like who?" asked Nicki.

John reached over and rested a rough and calloused hand on Nicki's shoulder. "Your father."

Nicki's body stiffened and a million different feelings shot through her arms, her legs, and her chest. A smile widened across her face and a wave of excitement coursed through her body. She sat up straight and leaned toward the old man, her eyes wide with curiosity. "You knew him?"

John chuckled. "Well, I should hope so. He was my son."

Nicki's stomach suddenly came alive with the fluttering of butterfly wings. "Wait, if—" She held a hand out and seemed to work everything out in her mind as she calculated the situation on her fingers. She lifted her hand and pointed at John. "Then you're my—"

John nodded and smiled.

Nicki's arms flew around the old man and squeezed tight, taking him by surprise.

"Ooh!" He wrapped an arm around Nicki and nuzzled his head into her hair before kissing her on the forehead.

"You're my grandpa." Nicki choked out her words and tears of joy streamed down her cheeks. She couldn't believe she had another grandpa. She'd only ever met one.

"Oh, Kiddo." It's all John could say as he mussed the hair on top of her head and kept his forehead pressed to her.

"Wait, so why didn't you come and find me? Why did I have to find you?"

John felt Nicki's body stiffen in his arms, and the anger building inside of her.

Nicki glared at her grandfather. "Why?"

"I didn't know, Kiddo. I didn't know about you. I swear. Of course I would've come." A look of guilt filled John's eyes.

"Then why did my mother hide you from me?" Nicki gritted her teeth and balled her hands into fists.

John reached down and lifted her chin with his index finger. Her face was red and blotchy. He hadn't seemed to have thought through all the possible outcomes of revealing the truth.

"She had her reasons. I promise. Okay?"

"Do you know my mom?"

John sighed loudly and he stared up at the ceiling. "Barely. I met her once."

"I want to know. What happened?"

"Look, Nicki, I—" He looked at the little girl who seemed to have the smarts of an adult. "I'm not sure what your mom wants you to know and I have to respect her wishes, okay? She may be waiting until you're older to tell you all of this."

"It's my life! This isn't fair! I deserve to know if I have a—" Nicki pointed at her grandfather and started to cry big fat wet teardrops which slowly melted the ice around John's heart.

His face paled watching his only granddaughter suffer in front of him.

"All I can tell you is that your father was in love with your mom. And they ran away to the city when they were very young—too young."

"Thanks, I knew that already. You're a great help." Nicki folded her arms over her chest.

John chuckled, even though it still looked as if sadness had overtaken him. Nicki had definitely inherited her father's sarcasm.

"I have an idea. Something you might be very interested in, as a matter of fact."

Nicki perked up a little and then narrowed her eyes. "I'm listening," she grumbled.

John belted out a laugh so loud it seemed to make the light from the fire flicker around the room more. "You are something else, you know that?"

"My mom tells me that every day." Nicki grinned.

"Well, this is top secret and you have to swear that you will not tell a single soul. Can you do that?"

"Maybe." Nicki glared, hiding a smile. She was a skillful negotiator.

John waggled his bushy silver eyebrows at her. "It has to do with that truck outside."

Nicki responded as soon as she heard the word "truck" and said, "I promise!"

John snickered. "Well, okay then. Follow me."

CHAPTER SEVEN

THE CURIOUS-LOOKING CHRISTMAS TRUCK

JOHN HELPED NICKI put on one of her father's old jackets. It engulfed her tiny body, but she hugged her small arms around it like it fit perfectly. They walked out through the door and toward the giant red truck that Nicki loved more than almost anything in the world.

John stopped her about halfway. "This is a very special truck, okay?"

"I know. I've seen it in pictures." Her mind raced as the sun began to set over the side of the mountains. She rattled off a zillion questions that popped into her head all at once. "It used to carry the Christmas tree to the city. Why doesn't it do that anymore? What happened to the trees? Did you know that hardly anyone cares about Christmas anymore? Did you know kids say Santa isn't real?"

"Whoa, easy there, Kiddo. Wow, you can ask a lot of questions fast."

Nicki shrugged. "Sorry, I ask questions when I get excited, or nervous."

John laughed and a foggy steam cloud puffed into the air in front of him. "That's okay. Nothing wrong with wanting to know things." He pulled a wool cap over Nicki's head and ears and then put one on his head as well. "It gets mighty cold when the sun goes down. Follow me."

They walked around to the driver's side door of the truck, where only hours before John had scared her half to death when she almost turned the key. He knelt down on the ground and put a hand on each of Nicki's shoulders. "This truck here—it's not an ordinary truck. It's part of your family history and legacy."

"I don't understand."

John smiled through his stringy beard. "This truck was built at the North Pole, by Santa Claus and the elves, many many years ago."

Nicki's eyes lit up and she gasped. "Really?"

John nodded. "Ooh yes. And there's more—" His eyes opened wide and his voice lowered to a whisper. "It comes alive when powered by the Christmas spirit. It's an amazing thing. It was built to carry the big trees down to the city."

"Wow!" Nicki stared at the truck in awe.

"There's more."

"Even more?"

John grinned. "Mmhmm. You see, the tree inspires the Christmas spirit in the city. But Santa also uses the tree as part of his navigation.

It's like a map. It gets him to all the houses around the world. I'm not sure how that part works, because he and the elves built it. It has something to do with radars and satellites and stuff. It's much more difficult for him to get around without it. But our family—" He pointed at himself, then at Nicki. "We're the drivers and caretakers of the truck."

Nicki smiled so hard she thought her face might get stuck that way. "Really?"

He nodded and leaned toward her. "It's a very, very important job." John looked away. "One that I haven't done very well. Ever since your father—" His voice cracked. "Umm, yeah."

"So, will I get to do it one day?"

John still couldn't look back at her. "I'm afraid not, Kiddo."

Nicki's face tightened. "But why? You said it's family."

"When they first built the truck, the elves told me the responsibility passes to the first-born son in each family."

Nicki's heart seemed to sink down into her stomach. "Th-that's not fair. Why can't a girl drive the truck?"

"Oh, Nicki." John tried to hug her but she pushed his arms away.

"The boys in my class were right all along. They told me a girl couldn't drive a truck, and I called them liars. But I was the liar!" She cried into the sleeve of her father's jacket.

Her heart ached and ached, because she wanted nothing in the world more than to drive the Christmas truck. For the first time in her life, she knew exactly what she wanted to do and exactly what she wanted to be, and yet it couldn't ever happen. And it was all because she was a girl.

"I'm sorry, Kiddo. Come over here." His eyebrows raised like he had an idea. "I can still set you up in the front seat and let you steer the wheel. Would that help?"

Nicki sauntered over. Her heart remained crushed by the news, but she couldn't pass up an opportunity to steer the Christmas truck. John lifted her onto the seat and Nicki's frustration slowly turned back to a grin. She stared through the window and imagined all the adventures the truck had seen, going up through the mountain to get the Christmas tree and then down into the city.

John sniffed the frigid night air. "Smell that, Nicki?"

Nicki inhaled a huge whiff. "Lots and lots of snow coming."

"Yep." John paused. "Okay, pretend to honk the horn once, and then we've gotta get inside. Tomorrow is a big day."

"What's tomorrow?"

"I have to go get the tree."

"You still get a tree? It's supposed to be a blizzard? And why haven't I seen the tree my whole life?"

"There's always a tree there. It's just a small one that I fit in the farm truck. I haven't been able to get the big rig to start since your father left."

"Did you put gas in it? You have to use diesel."

John laughed. "Oh, Kiddo. This truck doesn't run on gas."

"Huh?" Nicki canted her head to the side. "Well what makes it run?"

John winked. "Christmas spirit, like I told you."

CHAPTER EIGHT

A BEDTIME CHRISTMAS STORY

LATER THAT NIGHT, John tucked Nicki into a bed in a spare bedroom. "All right. Get some rest. Tomorrow I'll take you back down to Grant and Liz's before I head out." He kissed her on the forehead.

"Okay."

Her grandpa walked out of the room, but left the door cracked so that just a sliver of light peeked through. Nicki squeezed her eyes shut, but her mind came alive. Was it the Christmas spirit that had called her to the truck? Why did it have to be a boy that drove it? She dreamed of all the possibilities if she were only a boy instead of a girl. She could drive the truck and take a new tree to the city. Then everyone would believe and be happy again, and there would be so many lights and decorations. The Santa suit man would give food and toys to all the hungry kids.

A freezing, chill air whipped through the room, and it spoke gently in her ear. "Nicki."

She yanked the covers up over her head, frightened. The air chattered again.

"Come here."

Fear took hold of her body and chilled her bones, but she felt the pull from across the hall. The same force that led her to the truck.

Her grandpa had been gone for a short while and was probably downstairs making preparations for tomorrow. Nicki slipped out of bed slowly and her cold toes curled to grip the carpet.

She eased her way over to the door and peeked through.

A shiver ran up her spine and made the tiniest hairs on the back of her neck stand up.

"In here." The voice came from the room across the hall. It was like the scary movie she accidentally watched one time when her mom was sleeping. The person on the television kept walking into dark rooms when she shouldn't have. Nicki had yelled at the screen, but it didn't stop the woman. Something had jumped out and grabbed her. Nicki had screamed and then shut the movie off.

It's all Nicki could think about at the moment, something jumping out and grabbing her—but she crept quietly over to the room and turned the handle anyway.

When she walked inside she blinked twice and rubbed her eyes before recognizing her surroundings. The fear and creepy thoughts of some horrendous monster or bony skeleton hand grabbing her from the shadows left her body. Nicki's eyes lit up and a warmth rushed into her cheeks. She couldn't believe she didn't think to ask John about this room that she should have known existed. Nicki closed her eyes and inhaled a deep breath.

I'm standing in my father's room.

She opened her eyes and spun a full circle, enwrapped by her dad's pictures on all four walls—and there were trucks too. Sooo many trucks! More than Nicki had at her house even.

"Read me."

She whipped around, gazing in the direction of the voice's origin. Squinting in the low light she noticed a bookshelf full of Christmas stories. She walked over and picked out *Twas the Night Before Christmas*. Nicki opened it up and traced her dad's handwriting with her finger, only it looked like he was a child when he'd written it.

Nick's Favorite Book.

Nicki climbed into his old bed and started reading the words aloud, but she couldn't pronounce some of them very well. The corners of Nicki's mouth turned down and her eyes darted momentarily to a few pictures on the wall. She wished she had a picture of her and her dad. She'd always wanted one to remind her of him, but her mother didn't have any with Nicki in them.

Why can't you get this word right, Nicki? You're a good reader.

"K-k-kare-ch-ch-chife."

Nicki couldn't figure out how to say the word "kerchief." She stuttered and fumbled about, her tongue twisting each time she tried to say it. She balled her hands into fists. This was *her* dad's favorite book and she wanted to read all of it. Every last word.

"You shouldn't be in here!" John's voice boomed from the doorway.

Nicki slammed the book shut. "I'm sorry. I'm—"

John stormed through the door and glared.

Nicki held the book to her chest and cowered at his voice.

John's face softened, and he walked over to her. "No, no, I'm sorry, Kiddo. I'm just still getting used to all of this. I haven't opened this door in many years. It still hurts to see it."

"I-I didn't mean for all this to happen."

He smoothed a few wayward strands of Nicki's hair back behind her ear. "I know you didn't. And the word you're trying to say is *kerchief*. You say it curr-chiff. Scooch over."

Nicki smiled. She shuffled to the other side of the bed and her grandfather climbed in beside her.

"I should've put you in this room to begin with. It's where you belong. Now, let me see this here book." He whipped a pair of reading glasses out of the front pocket of his overalls and pushed them up over his nose. He squinted at the book through the lenses. "Ohh." He glanced over to Nicki. "Yep, this is a good choice for a Christmas story."

She knew he was teasing because he'd already told her the word kerchief and had to have known what she was reading, but she played along anyway.

"Is it?"

"Oh yeah. It's a Christmas classic." He handed it back over to her.

Nicki read the whole story from start to finish without making one mistake, and even said "kerchief" right. She swore her grandfather's beard grew less haggard and some of his wrinkles had disappeared from his face by the end.

"Will you read it to me, Grandpa?"

"Of course I will, Kiddo. You can't read this book too many times. It's just not possible."

They both smiled.

He started over from the beginning and Nicki's eyelids grew heavy. By page two she fell into a peaceful slumber, curled up next to John while he finished the story.

When he was done, he looked down and saw her tiny arms clinging around his waist and he smiled and rubbed her back. Some Christmas cheer, however small the amount was, seemed to have worked its way back into him.

Chapter Nine

The Dream

Nicki stood in front of the Christmas truck and a man worked under the hood. She could only see the backs of his legs while he was bent over. Staring at his faded blue jeans, and then down to a pair of old, worn work boots, she asked, "Hey Mister, are you fixing the truck?"

The man popped up from the engine and smiled at her. "As a matter of fact, I am."

She recognized him from pictures, not that she wouldn't have known otherwise. It was her father. Nicki smiled from ear to ear and he mussed the hair on top of her head. "You gonna stand there all day, or help out?"

"Yeah, what's going on around here? Put her to work! Ain't no free rides out here, Kid!"

Nicki jumped back, completely startled. Her face was ghostly white and she trembled all over.

Her father, Nicholas (or Nick as he told her to call him), laughed.

"D-did that t-truck just talk to me?"

"Yeah I did. No free rides around here. Only the tree gets a free ride. Know what I'm sayin', Nick?"

"Preach!" Nick replied. "No free rides."

Nick held out his fist and the truck lifted its front tire up and bumped it.

The headlights of the truck bounced around and focused on Nicki like a pair of bright eyes staring at her, and the grill opened and closed when it spoke.

"B-but you're a truck. How are you talking?"

"Neat, huh?" Nick raised his eyebrows up and down at Nicki, and he pulled a wrench from his toolbox.

"How though?"

"This one over here, Nick. She just ain't gettin' it, is she? Girlie Face, listen up. I ain't no regular truck, see? I was made by elves and Santa Claus. You think they just make normal ol' trucks up there at the North Pole? Pffft."

Nicki laughed. "You're funny."

"I'm funny. I'm funny. Ha ha ha. No!" He raised up and pointed a tire at her. "This is serious business here, Kid. I got a job to do, see?"

"He's right, Nicki. He does have a very important job to do."

Nicki knew she was dreaming, but she just couldn't wake up. She fought against it and stared up at her dad. He was so young and full of energy. His smile looked like hers when she would smile into her mom's makeup mirror. He had the same light blue eyes and sandy-blonde hair. When she looked at him more things about herself started to make sense. Things that made her think she was just weird before.

"And you have to take my job over one day. It's a family business. So you need to pay attention and become friends with SNOT over here." Nick pointed at the front of the truck.

The truck narrowed its headlights and appeared to glare at Nicholas. "Really, Nick? Reeeaally?"

Nicki giggled. "Your name is Snot?"

"Yeah, Girlie Face. See, the elves, and the jiggly man in the red jacket, and your father over there think they're comedians. Har har har, Nicholas. Hardy har har." The headlights whipped over to Nicki. "It stands for Santa's Networked Operations Tower. Hilarious, aren't they? Pffft!"

Nicki kept laughing and her father smiled. "Wait, what do you mean I have the family business to take over?"

"Well, who else is going to drive this truck when I'm gone? One day I'll be too old, like your Grandpa. The Christmas spirit fades the older we get. Especially when, well—sometimes things happen that cause us to lose it too. It's the strongest in children. They believe more than grown-ups are able to."

"Yeah, b-but I'm a girl."

SNOT and Nicholas both glanced to each

other and then back to Nicki. "So?" They both said it at the same time like she was from outer space.

"So the boys at school and then Grandpa— they umm—they told me girls can't drive trucks. Well, not Grandpa, he just said I couldn't drive this truck—SNOT."

"Oh sheesh, what is this the 1800s, Nicky Boy? You need to handle this here before I get filled with the spirit up in this joint and get all truckified on someone." SNOT lifted up one of his tires and pointed at Nicki.

Nicholas stopped what he was working on and walked slowly over to his daughter. He knelt on the ground so that their noses were only inches apart. "I don't have much time here with you. You already know that. You'll wake up soon." He clutched his daughter's face and beamed, his eyes never leaving Nicki's.

Her body warmed at her father's love for her, and how much they were alike. She definitely understood now where her love of trucks came from.

"I need you to listen to me, Nicki. If you don't remember anything else from your time with me, I want you to remember what I'm about to tell you, okay?"

"Okay, Daddy." She nodded.

"Nobody can ever tell you that you can't do something." He tapped his index finger lightly on her heart. "Except for you."

Nicki lunged at her Dad, wrapping her arms tight around his shoulders. A tingling sensation ran through her arms and legs down to the tips of her fingers and her toes. It filled her whole body, and she felt as if she might float off into the sky. Others might have said she couldn't drive a truck, but she always knew that she could. It was the greatest gift her Dad could've given her—hope.

"Seriously, what kinda backward stuff they teaching in schools these days, Nicholas? A girl can't drive a truck? Kafooey!" SNOT spit some oil out onto the ground through his grill. "That is all I have to say, my friends! Kafooey!" The headlights turned to Nicki. "You can drive me any time you want, Girlie Face."

"Aww, thanks, SNOT!" Nicki smiled.

His headlights lowered as if he was staring at the ground. "Can you call me like 'S' or something? I really don't feel like SNOT captures my true essence." He raised the driver's side front tire up like a hand to his chest, and a pair of metal eyelids closed over the headlights.

"Sure she can, SNOT!" Nicholas raised his voice when he said 'SNOT' and winked at Nicki.

"Keep it up, Funny Man. Keep it up! See what happens." SNOT narrowed his headlights at Nicholas. "See if we don't just go all happily hap hap bouncy bouncy up the mountain, and oops, what's that?" One of his front tires came forward in front of the grill as if he were covering up his mouth. He pretended like he was a damsel in distress, and tried to make his voice sound like a woman. "A flat tire you say? Ohhh, the horror. Ohhh, I'm just so sorry there, Master Nicholas. It's just so cold out here, and oh my gosh. The heater won't work either? I do declare! What a travesty that truly is, Sir! Oh yes, the blankets, I've got blankets. Oops! Ohhh my, I accidentally shot window cleaner all over them. Just trying to keep the windows nice and clean, Master Nicholas." He pointed a tire at Nick and bugged one of his headlights out. His voice returned to normal. "You try me, buddy. Just try me. I dare you to try me."

"You finished yet, SNOT?" Nicholas asked.

Nicki and her father burst into howls of laughter again.

"You guys are wrong, mannn. Just fix me up under the hood, okay? Nothing crazy, no new styles. I like my look the way it is, classic and refined." He wiggled his windshield wiper eyebrows up and down.

"You got it, buddy." Nicholas tapped on the hood, and then turned to Nicki and caressed her cheek. "It was so so incredible to finally get to talk to you. There's so much I want to say, but you need to be waking up soon."

"I don't want to ever wake up. I want to stay here with you and SNOT." Nicki sniffled and wiped a tear from the corner of her eye.

"I know, Kiddo. But you have to take care of my dad, your grandpa. He's in bad shape. And you need to make sure your mom is okay. Tell her to slow down and enjoy her time with you. She works so hard and it's because I can't be there." His shoulders slumped. "I just don't want her to miss out on all the good moments with you."

"I-I'll tell them, Daddy."

"And tell Grant and Liz hi for me. They are the best friends I ever had. We all knew each other since we were your age. Please stay in touch with them."

"I will. I promise."

"Come here." He held his arms out and Nicki raced into his embrace. Nicholas clutched the back of her head and kissed the top of it. Nicki's arms squeezed him into a tight hug. "I love you—" Nicholas's voice cracked and Nicki felt his tears soaking into her hair. "So much. I love you and your mother so very much. And I miss you every single day." He pulled away from Nicki and wiped his misty eyes. "But I am always watching you, okay? I am so proud of you, and I always will be, no matter what happens."

"I love you too, Daddy."

He pulled her back into another hug and Nicki had never thought anyone could ever make her feel as loved as her mother did, but she was wrong. This whole new side of her family she never knew about brought her so much joy.

"Remember what I told you. You can do anything."

Grrrdl grrrdl grrrdl.

His words quickly drowned in a thunderous beating sound, like a drummer pounding out a rapid rhythm. Nicki's eyes vaulted open and frames on the wall of her father's old room vibrated and rattled against the sheet rock.

Vroooooshhhh!

A shadow of something flashed by the window.

What in the world?

Nicki rubbed her eyes and leapt from the bed. Her feet landed flat on the warm carpet with a dull thud. She heard rustling outside and the jingling of bells behind muttered voices.

Nicki beamed at her father's boyhood picture on the wall by the door. She raced past it and flew down the stairs in a flash. The sounds from outside the house grew louder when she neared the main entrance to the house. She stopped and threw on the wool cap her grandfather placed on her head earlier, and then slipped into her shoes. Nicki shrugged on her father's old jacket—comforted after the dream from which she just awoke—and wrapped it securely around her petite body.

When she made it out into the yard she turned and looked. The truck trailer stretched past her, way beyond the house.

Then she saw it.

No, it can't be!

In front of Nicki sat a giant red sleigh that resembled a Viking ship more than something Santa would ride in, but something inside of Nicki just knew.

Santa!

A tingling sensation ripped through her whole body and Nicki froze in her tracks. She beamed at the sight in front of her, unable to do anything but stare. A reindeer cocked its head back in front of the sleigh and fuzzy brown antlers shot up in front of the big orange Harvest moon that lingered on the horizon above the city. A squeal caught in Nicki's throat and barely escaped.

They're as big as horses!

One of them yanked his head and one of the many wires attached to patches on their backs tightened and threatened to snap.

"Stop jerking, Comet!" A voice Nicki hadn't heard before was low and rumbly. "If we can just wire the Christmas spirit from the reindeer and tap their supply, maybe we can capture it into this battery."

"It'll never work," said SNOT.

"Santa?" Nicki called. She crawled under the trailer to the other side to dodge the reindeer.

"Nicki, you out here?" John got out from under the hood and walked around to her side of the truck. He smiled at Nicki.

"Pffft, you probably didn't tell that poor girl about me. Did ya? Did ya, Old Man?" SNOT chuckled.

"I thought she'd been through enough already. And nobody knew you were suddenly going to wake up in the middle of the night." Grandpa put a hand on the hood of the truck. "It is good to see you again, though."

"SNOT, you're awake!"

The headlights on the truck raised up toward the sky and then darted to her. The grill moved up and down with each word, just like in Nicki's dream, only this time it was real.

"Heyyy, how'd you know my name, Kid? What gives?"

John eyed Nicki curiously as well.

"I had a dream and you were real and talking! My daddy was there and was working on you."

Nicki turned to the other pair of legs bent over at the waist with his torso tucked under SNOT's hood.

"Dad?"

Nicki's eyes widened, but it was Giftavius who rose from under the hood.

Nicki looked at his red-striped socks and elf shoes that curled up to a point, and knew she should've realized it wasn't her dad before she'd said anything.

When Giftavius spoke, his face wrinkled and his teeth were pointy and shark-like. Nicki shrank away from him, despite her curiosity. She'd never seen an elf before.

"I'm sorry, Nicoletta. Your father was only part of your dream, I'm afraid."

He hopped down and walked toward her. Nicki sniffed in a huge breath of the cold air and it stung her nostrils. She didn't mind though.

"Soon, Kiddo." Her grandfather winked.

"Yep."

John smiled at her response. They both knew that the snow would start any minute.

Giftavius neared and stopped a few feet in front of Nicki. For the first time in Nicki's life she was taller than someone who was older than her, barely.

"Boy, I've got some energy now! Wooo! Did

you guys dump a Red Bull in my radiator or what?"

"You don't have a radiator. You are not a combustion engine. We have been over this, *SNOT*." Giftavius pointed to Nicki. "And it's because of her."

"Huh?" Nicki's grandpa and SNOT asked at the same time, then stared at one another and shrugged.

"The Christmas spirit is powerful in her. Can you not feel it?" Giftavius turned to the old man and the truck.

"Sure. Sure. I feel it." SNOT rolled his headlights when Giftavius wasn't looking.

Nicki glanced up at her grandfather then back to the elf. "My dad said, in my dream—he umm, he said that girls could drive the truck."

John started to speak. "Well now—"

Giftavius cut him off in the middle of his sentence. He reached out and cupped Nicki's rosy red cheek in his palm. He looked younger, like a child. His face had changed and now it was round and smooth. "Of course a girl can drive this truck. Especially one with a special gift like yours."

John glared at Giftavius. "You and the elves specifically told me that—"

"We told you it would be *your* first-born son. Not all first-born sons."

Nicki smiled a Cheshire-sized grin at Giftavius. "Really?"

"Oh yes, Nicoletta. This is what you were meant to do. It's in your bones."

"Why does he call me Nicoletta?" Nicki

stared at John who shrugged.

"Because that is your name, Child. It's a family name. Your father gave it to you for that very reason. Or do you not know your family's history?" Giftavius glared at John and then walked over and put an arm around Nicki.

"No, I don't. As far as I know, my name is Nicki Noel."

Giftavius shook his head. "Oh no, no. See, you are a descendant from the Claus bloodline. Your family was tasked with seeing to the City Christmas tree. Though it might seem small in the grand scheme of Christmas, it's an honor of the highest importance."

"Really? I mean, I knew the part about the tree and truck. But we're related to Santa Claus?"

"Oh yes. Your grandfather's name is John Klaussen." The elf nodded to John. "We changed it a little to misdirect suspicions, if any were to ever arise. Your father, however, was named Nicholas, in honor of Saint Nicholas himself."

"He's named after Santa Claus?" Nicki exclaimed.

"That's right. Santa Claus loved your father very much. And your father passed an Italian version of the name on to you. Nicoletta is a female version of Nicholas. The other tree that Santa uses to guide his sleigh is located in front of St Peter's Cathedral. Your father also loved Italian food. And ultimately, because you would one day be the driver of our beloved, SNOT."

"Still hate my name. Can we spruce it up a bit?" SNOT chuckled. "Get it? Spruce? Because that's what kind of tr—"

Giftavius and John both scowled at SNOT.

"Fine. Fine. Nobody has a sense of humor around this place. I swear." His grill closed tight and he made a motion with his tire zipping it shut.

Nicki chuckled. She looked up at the sky and saw a large fluffy snowflake floating above the trees and she followed it back and forth, all the way down. It landed across the bridge of her nose like the first snowflake always did. When it collided with her warm skin it melted off into a few drops of water that trickled down her cheeks. She giggled. Brutus walked over and licked the water from her cheeks, and she laughed once more.

John became overjoyed at the sight of his granddaughter smiling and laughing with Brutus.

Giftavius continued, "When your father fell in love with your mother, he didn't think he would be able to talk her into moving onto the mountain. It all happened so quickly for them. But he was willing to give up all of this, because he cared so deeply for her. They made plans, and ran away together to the city. Your father changed both of their last names, to signify a new beginning of life on their own. But he still kept behind some of the Christmas heritage by changing the name to Noel." Giftavius grinned and his teeth were no longer sharp and scary.

Nicki loved his striped socks that made his legs look like candy canes.

"It doesn't matter, Giftavius. We're still

doomed." John sniffed in the air and glanced over to him and Nicki.

"It's going to be a big one," Nicki said.

John nodded. "I can't take her out in a blizzard. Heck, we shouldn't go at all. It's dangerous."

"Yes." Giftavius nodded in agreement. "I'm afraid you're correct."

"Ohh, kafooey!" SNOT pretended to spit something out toward the woods. He made a loud sputtering sound that Nicki found quite funny. "She'll be with me, ya old codgers. Check it out."

Clank clonk!

Nicki heard gears grinding together. Two huge mechanical arms like those on Nicki's toy bulldozers—only much longer and wider—lifted from SNOT and rotated back toward the trailer.

"Whoa!" Nicki stared in awe while SNOT's large metal arms hooked onto a blade, and pulled it over the top of the cab. The blade finally landed in front of the truck on the pavement with a loud clank.

"Ya can't make the grade, without the blade." SNOT winked a headlight at Nicki and his grill smirked.

"No. It's too risky. Her mother definitely won't let her see me again if she knows I took her out in a blizzard to get a Christmas tree."

"I got every tool in the book. We're not getting stuck anywhere. Not to mention, you see my energy levels, right? She could power me for hundreds of years with that kinda juice." SNOT stared at Nicki for a brief moment and then turned to John. For the first time, he appeared serious. "John—" SNOT searched for the right words to say. "Nothing is gonna happen. I need you to trust me."

Giftavius looked back and forth at John and SNOT, then turned to the small girl drowning in her father's old jacket and wool cap.

Giftavius seemed very wise to Nicki, even if he looked like a little boy. He always thought everything through and then spoke very slowly and clearly.

"Sometimes, we must take risks, John. For the greater good. Sometimes it's not about keeping what we want and guarding it, regardless of events in the past." He glanced to Nicki. "Sometimes a fire that burns bright can smolder and burn out, if we don't allow it to breathe and give off the light it's supposed to. You of all men should know this." Giftavius turned to face John.

Nicki's grandfather removed his wool cap and clutched it in his hand. Nicki didn't like seeing him this way. He shook and stuttered, and she couldn't tell if it was from the cold air or the feelings inside of him when he looked at her.

"I-I know. But it's hard to let go. I just can't."

Nicki walked over and gave her grandpa a big hug. "I'll do whatever you want me to do, Grandpa." She took his hand in hers.

John smiled at his beautiful granddaughter.

"But there's no way I'll let my mom keep

me from you. I love you too much already."

John dropped to his knees in front of Nicki and pressed his forehead to hers. "I want you to go with us tomorrow. And I promise you I won't let anything happen to you. You *will* be safe, okay? SNOT wouldn't let you go if he thought you were in danger. We're going to bring the Christmas cheer back to the city. You and me, Kiddo."

SNOT faked a loud cough.

"And you too, SNOT." John hugged Nicki as tightly as he possibly could. "I love you too, Kiddo."

Nicki smiled at her Grandfather and stared curiously, convinced that a few more of his wrinkles had disappeared and that his beard had grown in fuller and whiter. "It's time, Grandpa."

"Yep."

They both looked up into the black night sky, and the snow started to fall.

And it fell fast.

CHAPTER TEN

THE JOURNEY UP THE MOUNTAIN

WHEN NICKI WOKE up the next morning she could already feel the presence of the snow. The light was incredibly bright that shone through the window of her dad's old bedroom. She'd fallen asleep under the same covers that he once slept under, and somehow she felt like she knew him better because of it.

Nicki had pulled the blinds up on the window the night before because she knew she'd want to stare at the snow in the morning. She always loved looking at the snow that fell during the night.

She hopped from the bed and skipped toward the sunlight.

"Wowww!" One of her cheeks and her right hand pressed up against the cold pane of glass.

A large blanket of thick white covered everything as far as she could see. It reminded her of the puffy white marshmallows she enjoyed in her hot cocoa. Her head tilted up and she continued watching the large round flakes fall from the sky.

She threw on her jeans, truck shirt, and her father's jacket, then skipped to the stairs and ran down them. Nicki yanked on her shoes, pulled on her wool cap and wrapped a plaid scarf she found in the closet around her neck.

"Here goes nothin'."

She pulled the front door open. Fresh snow that piled up nearly to her knee greeted her. It sparkled for miles. The cold wind bit at her face, but she didn't care. She leapt out into the snow, her feet planting firmly into two large, powdery holes. Reaching back, she shut the door and waded out into the yard where SNOT sat idling. Puffs of steam came up out of the silver pipes jutting out of his hood.

He's so silly, Nicki thought to herself. It had to be for show because he didn't have a normal engine, and Nicki knew all about truck engines.

Brutus hopped along out in the yard, kicking up white clouds of dust in his wake. Nicki stared at how beautiful he was with his thick, fluffy coat and ornery face, jumping and playing in the fresh snow.

John walked around the corner of SNOT and he didn't look nearly as happy as Brutus. In fact, quite the opposite. "Nicki, there's just no way. We can't get up the mountain in this." He stared around at the sky and glanced worriedly at the landscape.

"Nonsense! We got her with us!" SNOT pointed a tire right at Nicki.

She grinned sheepishly.

Nicki couldn't wait to hop inside the truck and actually go for a ride this time, even if it was through a foot of ice and snow. She knew SNOT would never put her in danger, and that her grandpa was just worried about her.

"No giving up now. We have to do it! It'll be safe," said SNOT.

John hesitated, and held his fist up to his mouth. He seemed to be thinking everything over and talking himself out of it.

"It'll be fine, Grandpa. I promise!"

Nicki's excitement pushed all of her fears aside for the moment.

"I have to call Liz and Grant. They think you're going to their house today. They'll be worried sick."

"Okay." Nicki nodded and she hopped and skipped after her grandfather.

"Come on." He waved Nicki into the house. "You need to come in and warm up for a minute."

Nicki kicked her shoes on the rug in front of the door and watched the big chunks of white slush fall off onto the warm rug and turn to mush. Her grandfather pulled his cap from his head and grabbed the phone. The stairs were next to her and she imagined her dad running down them on Christmas morning and then across the living room to the tree. She hadn't asked what happened to her grandmother, even though there were a few pictures here and there. Her grandpa already seemed on edge enough when she asked about her dad. She figured in time she'd get her grandmother's story.

"I don't have time to explain but I need to take her with me. I promise it's safe."

John paced back and forth through the house, but stopped when he noticed Nicki watching from the entryway.

"I know it sounds dangerous, but it's not. I swear. She's my granddaughter. I wouldn't put her in harm's way. I'm telling you. Hello? Hello?"

Nicki noticed that John squeezed the phone so hard she could see the whites of his knuckles. He turned to face her and then sat the phone down gently. "Well, that didn't go over so well, Kiddo. Maybe it's best if you don't go. You can ride in the truck down to Liz and Grant's, and then I'll drop you off to wait out the storm with them."

"No!" Nicki stomped her feet again, but this time there wasn't any snow on her boots to come off. She didn't usually throw fits when she didn't get her way, but this was different. Liz and Grant must not have understood how important what they were doing was. "You heard Giftavius last night. I have to go or SNOT may not make it. What if something happens to him, or to you?"

Grandpa scratched his head and sighed while staring up at the ceiling. Nicki's eyes started to sting and the bridge of her nose tingled. Not in a good way. Why did it have to snow like this? On this one day? It wasn't fair.

"I finally found out what I was made to do. And I never ask for anything, ever. I just want to help bring Christmas back to the city. You don't live there, but it's cold and mean and people are hateful. It's horrible, Grandpa." She hugged her arms tight around his right leg. "It's just awful."

John nodded to his granddaughter. "All right."

Nicki's head whipped up to meet his eyes. They were icy and blue, but somehow warmed her heart. He stared at her with a look of determination, and any bit of fear inside of her disappeared.

"We'll do it. But Grant is going to call your mother. And I have a feeling it won't be good when we get finished."

"She won't be able to be mad when she sees what happens. I just know it."

John patted Nicki on the head. "We'll see, Kiddo."

❄ ❄ ❄

"You ready for this?"

John sat with his hands on the steering wheel. Nicki buckled up in the passenger seat. She turned and nodded.

"All right, SNOTTY Boy, let's do it."

"I ain't SNOTTY Boy and we have to work on my name." SNOT paused and then chuckled. "But okay. Let's do it! You have the coordinates?"

"Right here in my pocket." John pulled out

the envelope the elves had given him during their meeting in the dark room and he cracked the red Santa wax seal. He typed some numbers from the paper into a screen on SNOT's dashboard.

The engine under the hood roared, and John winked at a beaming Nicki.

Putt.

Putt.

Sputter.

Kerthunk.

The engine died.

"What? How? Why?" John looked around the console and tapped his palm on the dash. "Talk to me, SNOT."

"I don't know what happened. I felt great and then—" SNOT made a loud yawning sound. "I'm just so tired. Must have sleepy now." He purred contently like it was time to take a nap.

"No. No. You can't go to sleep. We have to get the tree!"

"We can just like, do it tomorrow and stuff."

They were losing SNOT, fast.

John glanced over to Nicki. "Trade me seats."

"Huh?" Nicki's eyes widened and her eyebrows shot up her forehead.

"You heard me. Maybe you need to be driving. Gotta take the reins someday soon anyway." John looked around at all the snow on the ground and shrugged. "Heck, why not? Don't worry, SNOTTY does all the work for you."

Nicki hesitantly unbuckled her safety belt and they traded places. Fear and happiness both swirled through her like a cyclone.

John reached over and rested his big, brawny hand on her shoulder. "Just give him a little wake up call." He nodded at the horn and winked.

Nicki's mouth formed a wry smile. She held up two hands and then slammed them down on the steering wheel.

Braaaahhhhhh!

SNOT shot to life and his engine screamed under the hood.

"Wooo!" The cabin shook to life. "That's the stuff right there, now! Wooo! I'm wide awake." The lights on the dashboard flickered and danced around. "Oh, we got us a new captain in here now, do we? Let me tell ya somethin', Captain Nicki. What you have inside of you is better than a whole lake of coffee. That's some mighty potent Christmas cheer. A hundred percent pure. Wooo!"

Nicki laughed and laughed, and John's face glowed bright red as well. His shoulders bounced up and down and he smiled so big he showed Nicki his teeth.

"All right, folks. Buckle up. SNOT's running the show. It's time to find us a Christmas tree. Wooo!"

SNOT made the horn blare a few more times, and the large mechanical arms came over the top of the truck. They lowered down in front of them where Nicki and John could see through the windshield.

Thud!

The giant blade that would push the snow out of the way hit the ground and SNOT surged forward, pulling the large trailer behind.

Nicki looked into one of the rearview mirrors. "Stop!" she cried.

SNOT threw on the brakes, and Nicki and her grandfather lurched forward into their seatbelts.

"What is it, Nicki?" John stared over at her like she was a crazy person.

Nicki opened the door and leaned as far out as she could with the seatbelt strapped to her. "Come on, Boy!"

Sssprrrtttt.

Nicki tried to whistle but it sounded like someone learning to spit for the first time.

Brutus came thundering through the snow.

"You're gonna spoil him." John snickered.

"We can't save Christmas without Brutus." She looked down at Brutus. He stood there, wagging his tail back and forth. "Well come on!" She patted the seat and he leapt up onto the floorboard.

Nicki giggled and Brutus squeezed past her legs and hopped up next to John's window, shoving him toward the middle.

"Just sit wherever you want. Geez."

"We good to go now that the beast is on board?" asked SNOT.

Brutus growled at the dash.

Nicki couldn't stop laughing.

"Sorry, I meant no disrespect, Sir Beast Klaussen."

"Yeah, we're good. Take us to the tree." Grandpa scrubbed a hand through Brutus's fur and patted him on the back three times like he always did.

"Hey, Nicki?"

"Yeah, SNOT?"

"Do me a favor up there and think about some hot cocoa and mistletoe, will ya?"

"Sure." Nicki squinted her eyes and pictured herself back at home with her mom. She had hot cocoa in a mug with marshmallows, and some mistletoe hung up over the entryway where Amanda always put it.

"Wooo! That's what I'm talkin' about!" SNOT plowed forward down the driveway. "You think all the Christmas thoughts you want!"

They cut through the snow with ease, and even though Nicki held onto the wheel, SNOT navigated the truck around the bends and curves.

They pulled down the road where Liz and Grant lived. Both of them stood out in the driveway.

"Stop for a second," John said. He lowered his window as the truck slid to a halt.

The snow continued to dump on top of them from the sky and Liz and Grant held a hand up to their foreheads just to be able to see.

"I'm sorry, but she has to go with me. I can't drive the truck!" Nicki's grandfather had to yell for anyone to hear over the engine.

"Amanda called the police! They're going to send out search parties and rescue teams! There will be big trouble, John! I get it, I just don't want to see anyone get hurt! You sure you don't want to leave her with us?" Grant hollered from the driveway.

"If I could, I would. The truck goes to sleep if I'm behind the wheel."

"I'm fine, I promise!" Nicki yelled from the driver's seat.

Liz looked like she might pass out from shock. Like she couldn't believe any of this was happening.

"We'll be okay. I swear. Tell Amanda sending search parties is only going to put more people in danger. They don't have a machine like we've got to make it through the snow."

"I'll tell her, but I don't think she'll listen!"

"All right. Well tell her I'm sorry. It's the only way."

SNOT started to pull away and Nicki could hear Liz hollering at Grant about letting her go. It made Nicki sad to think she'd caused them to argue, but she knew in her heart she was doing the right thing. Her mother would see that, eventually—maybe.

Grandpa stared over at Nicki and then looked back at Liz in the mirror. "Maybe you should stay here, Nicki."

"Grandpa—" Nicki leaned over and gripped his hand. "It'll be fine."

He nodded with hesitation. SNOT pulled away and Nicki watched Liz and Grant grow small and disappear in the rearview mirror.

For the next hour, SNOT cut through the snow like a hot knife through butter. He was supercharged with Christmas spirit and John kept repeating, "I've never seen him like this before."

Nicki held on to the wheel and bounced up and down as they twisted and turned up the mountain roads. The snow grew higher and higher around them, but it didn't faze them at all. SNOT never even slowed down. He was built by the elves and Santa Claus to do this very thing, and he was very good at it.

Roosh roosh roosh, fwoo fwoooo!

The mountain rumbled beneath Snot's tires and Nicki's eyes widened when she heard a steam whistle blast in the distance.

"Oh, Nicki. Will you look at that—"

Nicki glanced to the mountainside, past her grandfather and through the window. Her skin tingled and tiny goosebumps pebbled up and down her arms.

"Wow! Even I've never seen it before." SNOT slowed to match its pace and seemed just as awestruck as Nicki and John.

The giant black train ripped up the side of the mountain, cutting through wisps of foggy steam in the middle of the trees that danced and swirled in the wind. Snow kicked up into a fine, powdery dust and glimmered around the thick metal bars of the pilot that hovered mere inches from the ground and seemed as if they might plow into the earth. Nicki's eyes roamed the powerful black beast that looked forged from cast iron and from a different world entirely.

Roosh roosh roosh!

Black bars connected to wheels on the old steam locomotive, and pistoned back and forth, churning it forward up the mountain faster than any train Nicki had ever seen before.

"Look at the steam, Grandpa."

Nicki nodded to the tall, wide stack that sat atop the powerful motor and shot magnificent puffy clouds of steam into the snowy wind with a loud and distinct whistle.

"I see it."

"Wait, where are the tracks?" Nicki gazed out beneath the ghost-like train, where the wheels usually connected to the track, but the round metal spun in the air and glided effortlessly across the ground.

"It doesn't need any. It's one of ours."

Nicki's nose crinkled at her grandfather's words as the train lurched across the landscape ahead in the distance.

It pulled so many black box cars that Nicki thought they might wrap and curl all the way down to the bottom of the mountain.

"One of ours?"

John and SNOT both chuckled.

Just then, the caboose appeared, bright red and beautiful—a sharp contrast against the mighty black convoy. A man with a thick black moustache that curled at the ends walked out on the deck and gazed at SNOT, Nicki, John, and Brutus. Nicki squinted her eyes, and made out a conductor's uniform that had to be eighty years old or more—a suit, tie, and cap.

"His name is Tom, but we call him Pep. And it's a kepi." John smiled.

"What is?"

"The hat he's wearing."

Nicki glanced back to the conductor who leaned over the railing attached to the deck. He held up a thumb in the air and smiled. Nicki and Grandpa returned the gesture. The man waved to Nicki and her jaw dropped when she noticed his pointy ears that poked out the side of his cap.

"Did—did you see?"

"Yep." John glanced over to his granddaughter with a huge grin. "Hopefully, someday we'll take a ride on it. It has a long journey ahead."

Nicki stared back through the window, and the train—along with Pep—faded into the dense snow and dissipated as if it were a foggy mist.

"Wait, you've ridden on that?" Nicki barely contained herself while she asked the question.

John reached over and rubbed Nicki's head. "Oh yes. You have a lot to learn about our family."

Nicki sat holding SNOT's wheel with a sheepish grin plastered to her face.

"It's right up here around the corner. You guys ready?" SNOT asked, snapping Nicki out of her fantastical daydream.

John nudged Nicki with his elbow. "You ready to see it?"

"More than anything." Nicki gazed ahead at the snow. The big flakes seemed to head right for her and then curve up over the windshield at the last second. Barren trees lined the road on both sides, and white powder clung to their wobbly branches.

Nicki and Grandpa both leaned to the left as SNOT lugged the trailer around a corner, the force pulling them toward Nicki's side of the truck. When SNOT straightened, John watched Nicki's face as she saw the Christmas tree for the first time.

She gazed high up in the sky with rosy red cheeks and wide sparkly eyes and gasped.

"It's beautiful."

CHAPTER ELEVEN

O' CHRISTMAS TREE

IN A FIELD along the right side of the road, still a ways off in the distance, the tree towered above everything that surrounded it. It was so tall in fact that Nicki had to lean forward and look up through the windshield to see the very top of it. Brutus barked and pressed his snout against the window of the door.

"It's perfect." Nicki continued to gawk at the majestic tree in front of her.

"I've missed this." John scratched Brutus behind the ears. "You think it'll get old, or you'll get used to it. But you never do. It still takes my breath away every single time I see it." He reached over and smothered Nicki's hand with his own.

Nicki's cheeks grew pink and rosy. Her grandfather stared at her once more while she looked out at the tree, taking in every little reaction.

The branches grew out wide at the bottom of the tree and then slowly narrowed all the way up to the tip top where it formed a point. From a distance, it looked like a large dark green arrow that might stab into the clouds. The snow still fell from sky to earth and covered everything in sight with smooth, rolling waves of white.

SNOT continued to plow right through anything in front of him. The sound of the snow beating against the blade and then shooting out to the side of the road filled Nicki's ears. It created a comforting melody that made her feel safe and secure.

"Almost there, guys." SNOT still sounded like he was loaded with Christmas cheer.

Nicki had grown used to the growl of SNOT's engine so much so that it was like a steady hum in the background, providing a rhythm for the songs the plow created against the snow.

When Nicki thought the tree couldn't seem any larger, it grew tenfold in her field of vision. She could see it more clearly now through the whipping snow as they neared. Clouds of fine white powder swooshed and swished around the tree and the branches shook wildly from the force of the wind. They were dark green and thick, and snow weighed them down from every angle. The large white deposits on the branches reminded her of icing on the cinnamon rolls her mom sometimes made her for breakfast.

"Pulling in," said SNOT.

"No need to be snotty about it." Grandpa nudged Nicki with an elbow to her ribs and she grinned. Brutus barked his approval at the joke.

"Laugh it up, in there. Ya give someone a first-class ride to the greatest Christmas show on the planet, and this is how they repay you."

The dashboard lights glowed brighter every time SNOT spoke as if he were in the truck with them. His voice echoed over the speakers.

SNOT slid to a slippery halt in front of the Christmas tree and the music of the churning snow and roaring engine slowed down and then stopped.

"We don't have much time. How quick can we get this done?" John leaned forward and tapped on the dash.

"Wait, wait. Oh no, this isn't good. John can you hop out? I need to have a friendly chat with you in private."

John's smile disappeared from his face. "Sure. Be right there." He turned to Nicki. "I'll be right back. Don't fiddle with anything."

"Don't worry about me, Grandpa. I'll be good." Nicki continued to lean way forward and gaze up at the tree. She could barely make out the top now that they were almost directly beneath it.

John opened his door and hopped down into the thick snow that was at least two feet deep at that point. He waded around to the front of the truck where Nicki could still see him, but she couldn't hear what was going on.

Nicki's grandfather wiped some snow from his face. He held a hand out and cupped it to his cheek to block the blowing snow that whipped up off the surface. Nicki watched the snow twirl in little eddies and shiver across the bright white ground. She watched Grandpa's lips moving, but she couldn't figure out what he was saying to SNOT.

"I picked up some radio activity. I didn't want to say anything in the cabin or play it."

"What is it?" John asked.

"There's a search and rescue team looking for—well, you know. They issued an amber alert for Nicki."

"They think I kidnapped her?" John stared up through the windshield at Nicki's innocent, curious expression. Guilt pounded his gut like a sledgehammer. He knew he might not ever get a chance to visit or see his granddaughter again after today. The thought of going to jail hadn't occurred to him, though. He clutched his palms to his head and kicked at the snow. "This isn't right. It's just not right. I just got her back in my life. I should've made her stay with Liz and Grant. I'm so stupid!"

"You hear that?" SNOT interrupted.

John stepped away from the truck's engine

and cupped a hand to his ear. The faint sound of a helicopter propeller cut through the whooshing wind and the crackling branches of the Christmas tree.

"They have a chopper out here in this weather? Gah, how can they be so, so—"

"Dumb?" SNOT asked.

"Yes! Dumb! Dumb! Dumb!" He looked up at Nicki once more. He waved and faked a smile for her and she waved back, then pointed up at the tree and grinned. He sighed. "I might as well enjoy what time I have with her."

The front of the truck moved up and down like SNOT was nodding in agreement. "Yep."

"All right, Old Buddy. Like the old times?"

"Rock 'n roll, Johnny! Rock 'n roll." The headlights glanced up to the tree. "The bigger they are, the more Christmas cheer they bring. That's what they say, right?"

"Indeed." John held his hand up when he walked by and the passenger side tire moved up into the air to give him a high five. "Let's do it!"

John climbed back into the cabin.

"Everything okay, Grandpa? You looked upset." She stared with worried eyes at her grandfather.

Flakes of snow hung suspended, caught in his beard like a spider web. He reached over and caressed the side of her cheek and then pushed a couple of strands of hair back behind Nicki's ear and up under her wool cap.

"Everything is perfect, Kiddo. You're about

to see something incredible. Are you ready?"

"Oh yeah!" Nicki laughed and clapped.

"Let's get this show on the road, SNOT!"

"Thought you'd never ask." SNOT revved up the engine and it roared against the sharp wind. His tone grew serious for the first time that Nicki could remember.

"All right. I'm going to back us up and let you guys out to watch, and then I'm going to put this Christmas tree where it belongs. Right back there on my trailer."

"Woo!" Nicki squealed.

Her grandfather laughed. He couldn't remember the last time he laughed and smiled so much. The cheer and happiness that the tree would bring the city, Nicki brought to her grandfather. Any time he looked at her face, all of his guilt and worries vanished.

The blade lifted in front of them through the windshield and shot overhead. Nicki glanced to one of the rearview mirrors that hung outside the window. SNOT extended the arms all the way past the rear of the trailer and the blade hammered the ground back in the distance.

"Already got some build up behind us. Hang on."

John and Nicki lurched forward when SNOT reversed away from the base of the tree. Once they'd backed up about a hundred feet, SNOT threw on the brakes, shoving their backs into the seat this time.

"Sorry. In a hurry. Didn't mean to jerk you guys around."

"Yeah yeah." John winked again at Nicki.

"Keep it up, Old Man. Keep 'em comin'. We'll see who's laughing later."

Nicki snickered. "I still love you!"

"Why thank you. Thank you very much, Nicki."

Nicki tried to wink back at her grandpa. Her wink needed some work, seeing as the whole side of her mouth opened when she tried to do it.

John couldn't stop smiling at his granddaughter.

"Even if your name is *SNOT*!"

John burst into laughter with Nicki.

"Oh, ohhh! I see how it is, Nicki. You did me wrong, Girlie Face!" SNOT chuckled, and cold air blasted John and Nicki from the vents.

Nicki squealed and dove into her Grandpa's lap. John laughed. "Okay, fine. You made your point."

Lights flickered and warm air replaced the cold.

Nicki sat up and whispered in her Grandpa's ear, "Bad SNOT."

John grinned at Nicki.

"You two done? I've got work to do."

"Yep, let's do it," John said.

"About time."

"Hang on, Nicki. I'll come around and get you. You're gonna wanna see this."

John hopped out of the truck and waded around through the snow. He opened Nicki's door and she jumped into his arms. Brutus followed after her. They all backed away from the truck and John threw SNOT a salute.

"This is what it's all about."

John whooped and hollered, "Bring her home!"

SNOT's headlights narrowed and the grill looked like it was gritting it's teeth. The engine purred and then exploded as the headlights seemed to expand.

"You're a beautiful, mighty tree."

SNOT's arms slowly lifted back overhead and then down in front of the truck. The blade landed flush with the ground in front of SNOT and he rocketed forward into the snow, hammering through each gear with a determined glare. White clouds of snow blasted across the field in SNOT's wake.

"Crane engage!" he screamed.

SNOT veered sideways when it appeared he might run head-first into the tree. He skidded with the elegance of an ice skater stopping on the ice. A giant piece of metal jutted from the trailer into the sky like SNOT had sprouted a tail.

"Grandpa look! Look!"

"I see it, Kiddo. I see it!"

The crane extended up into the sky until it was higher than the tree. It swayed back and forth in the wind. SNOT huffed and puffed and the tail started to spin and spin. A hook circled in a tight loop. It was attached to a steel cable.

"YEE HAWW! ROPE 'EM COWBOY!" SNOT's tail heaved the hook toward the top of the tree like it was casting a fishing pole. The hook wrapped around the branches at the top of the Christmas tree and latched onto the thick steel cable.

Once secured, SNOT screamed, "SAW!"

One of the huge arms shot out from the side of the truck and a gigantic rotating saw blade screamed as the sharp teeth cut through the air. It was so loud that Nicki had to cover her ears with her hands. The arm extended out until it was lined up with the tree, then rotated parallel to the ground before making contact with the trunk.

"What kind of tree is it, Grandpa?"

"It's a Norway Spruce. They usually only grow in Europe, but a few of them can be found around here. The elves and Santa Claus have a team that monitor them in different areas."

"Norway Spruce, huh?" Nicki stared at SNOT as his giant blade sawed through the trunk of the tree.

SNOT grimaced and groaned as a shower of sawdust flew from the blade out onto the surface of the snow.

There was a cracking sound, and the ground rumbled as the blade made it all the way through. The crane wobbled when it absorbed the weight of the tree.

Nicki couldn't stop smiling. There it was, hanging in the air suspended above the snow. The metal crane creaked and groaned.

"This is the biggest one I've ever seen, Nicki. It has to be at least 90 feet tall."

Nicki couldn't speak. She just stood there and marveled at the tree.

John put his arm around his

granddaughter's shoulders. They both stood silent for a few seconds, the young girl and the old man, both with the same awestruck glimmer in their eyes.

SNOT's crane tail slowly rotated back. With one quick motion the tree yanked sideways and landed perfectly on the trailer. It bounced up and down a couple of times, shaking everything. The neck of the crane whipped back and forth and the hook unraveled and released the tree. It shot back to the top of the crane as if spring-loaded. The tail lowered down into SNOT and somehow disappeared like magic.

Nicki didn't question where it went, or how it fit back into the truck. She just simply believed.

Large leather straps dropped from the side of the trailer and snaked their way around the Norway Spruce with minds of their own.

"Tighten 'er down!" SNOT hollered at the belts. At least twenty of them cinched tight around the tree. A few snaps and crackles filled the air when the huge branches scrunched together. Once secured on the trailer, the beautiful spruce snuggled in and fit perfectly on SNOT's bed.

SNOT threw the truck into reverse and whipped back around, the blade clearing all the new snow falling in front of him. He pulled up next to Nicki, Brutus, and her grandfather.

"You guys coming, or what?"

Nicki looked up and down the entire length of the trailer and nodded. "Oh yeah."

CHAPTER TWELVE

THE TREK DOWN THE MOUNTAIN

THEY JUMPED BACK up into the cabin. SNOT panted heavily and his voice grew tired and weary.

"What's wrong, SNOT? You okay?" Nicki's voice held a tone of concern, and she patted on the steering wheel.

"Woo! I'm good now! You left the front seat and I lost some juice. Almost used it all up with that behemoth on the trailer, but it was too dangerous to have you in the truck while I took down the beast."

"Oh. That makes sense," said Nicki.

Grandpa nodded. Brutus barked to add his approval.

"Well, I've gotcha now and I'm all jacked up

on cheer. Let's get going. Wooo!"

They took off on the road, heading back down the mountain with the huge tree strapped to the trailer.

They followed the same route they'd taken to get there, but everywhere they'd plowed on the other side of the road was already filled in with fresh snow.

Nicki inhaled a large breath of air through her nose. "It's not gonna stop anytime soon."

Grandpa sniffed the air too. "Yep."

They went down the mountain like a sidewinder snake, cutting back and forth on the old country roads.

"I'm sorry you have to hear this, Nicki. But I need us to be prepared." He flipped on the radio and SNOT tuned to the station where he'd heard the news earlier.

"Breaking news, the truck was spotted close to the top of Mount Sinter for a brief moment but the snow has made it almost impossible for rescue teams to see. The missing girl is identified as Nicki Noel. Her mother, Amanda, reported her as missing to police just a few hours ago, saying that her daughter had been kidnapped."

"Kidnapped?" Nicki shrieked. "What's going on?" She whipped around to face her grandfather.

"It's nothing, okay?" He reached for her arm. "People are just worried about you. That's all."

"But I haven't been kidnapped. Why is she

doing this?"

"Calm down, Kiddo. She's just concerned, okay? It'll be fine."

John gulped while the news continued to play.

"The suspected kidnapper is John Klaussen. He's believed to be the girl's grandfather. They were last seen driving up the mountain in a red truck used to haul the city Christmas tree to town, though authorities believe they may be headed back by now. If you see them please steer clear and alert the police department at once."

Nicki shook her head. "This is crazy."

"Let's just focus on getting the tree to town and having a good time. We'll deal with it when it happens."

"Hang on!" SNOT yelled and threw on the brakes.

They slid on the snow-packed road. Nicki and John's seatbelts tightened so hard it yanked them back to the seat. Grandpa had Brutus wrapped up in his arms so that he didn't fly into the dashboard.

A cloud of snow shot up in the air, and they couldn't see anything through the windshield. They finally slid to a stop.

Nicki and her grandfather both panted, their chests heaving up and down with each breath. John's hands flew over to Nicki and patted her down. She stared at his frightened face while he frantically wrapped his arms around her.

"Are you okay? Are you hurt?" His arms quivered against her. "WHAT ARE YOU DOING, SNOT?" he screamed.

"I-I just—"

The white powdery mist finally disappeared and they saw the problem.

A large tree branch had fallen and was blocking the road in front of them. Without it being moved, there was no way they could pass and make it to the city.

"Sorry—just—SNOT, I'm—" John released Nicki and she stared up at his face, frightened.

"It's okay. I understand." SNOT's dejected voice filtered through the speakers.

"Grandpa, are you okay?"

"It's nothing, Nicki. He'll be fine."

John shook his head and looked down at Nicki's trembling bottom lip. He sighed, and hugged her gently this time. "I'm sorry, Kiddo."

Nicki didn't want to upset him more. She wanted him back to his usual, happy self. "It's okay. I'm fine, I promise."

John leaned back and smiled. "Just got scared for a second. Old men can get scared too sometimes." He turned to the dashboard. "SNOT, pull out your saw and chop that thing up."

"Will do, Boss!" The truck shook and wobbled, and the motor from the saw whined before the sound faded away.

"What's wrong, SNOT?"

"I don't know. The saw is stuck. It won't engage."

"This can't be happening," John muttered.

"What are we going to do?" Nicki glared out at the branch in the street.

SNOT tried again and once more the motor hummed and then clanked and clonked to a halt.

Nicki glared at the road, trying to think of anything that could move it. "Can we just drive through?"

"It could be really dangerous and we could skid off the road," SNOT said.

Nicki looked past the branch and there was a curve right after.

"We can't get past it. This is what it comes to." John threw up his arms.

Nicki sat still thinking through the problem at hand. She gripped the steering wheel and SNOT jolted. The whole cab of the truck wobbled.

"What a rush!"

Within seconds a light bulb went off in Nicki's head. "Get ready to try the saw again, SNOT. Do it when I say." She smiled at John.

"What are you thinking, Kiddo?"

"I don't know. I'm going to try something." She gripped the steering wheel tightly once more and focused on the saw's motor. She thought about the tree going up and all of the city decorated for Christmas. Then she thought about the reindeer and the sleigh and Giftavius and Santa Claus. She fixated on all of the memories and ideas she had about anything which brought her Christmas cheer—lights, hot cocoa, snowflakes, carols, and more.

"Wooo! Wooo!" SNOT trembled as he absorbed all the cheer filling his fuel tanks. "That's the good stuff!"

Nicki kept focusing and then shouted, "Okay, now!"

SNOT tried the saw and it flew out to the side and the blade started to hiss in the cold air.

"Yes!" John pumped his fist and then shook Nicki by her shoulders. "Saw that thing up!"

SNOT moved the saw out and cut the branch up into smaller pieces like it was nothing. Sparks flickered through the cloud of snow and sawdust when it accidentally hit the pavement. SNOT used the arm to push the branches out of the way and down into the ditches on each side.

They drove past and John couldn't stop smiling at Nicki. She grinned and bounced in the seat as they sped down the hill on the way to the big city. When they reached the bottom of the mountain, the snow stopped falling. Nicki and John laughed at one another for what seemed forever.

They peered out at the skyline.

"Well, I guess this is it." Nicki stared straight ahead.

John glanced to Nicki and then back out at the buildings. He nodded. "Yep. Let's show this city what Christmas is all about."

CHAPTER THIRTEEN

FUN IN THE CITY

Two young boys stood on a street corner next to their parents when they spotted the bright red truck and the huge tree that seemed to stretch for miles.

"Whoa! Look!"

They whooped and hollered while the truck rumbled slowly down the street. The boys tugged at their parents' coats and said, "Look Mom! Look Dad!"

The horn of the truck blasted twice for the boys who pumped their arms up and down. When the truck was no more than fifty feet away their jaws dropped and they stared up at the larger-than-life vehicle in disbelief.

Nicki sat up straight in her seat and waved at the boys. She honked the horn twice more for them, but they stood still as statues, completely stiff and silent. It was the two boys from Nicki's class who had told her that girls couldn't drive trucks and that Santa Claus wasn't real.

"I guess they learned their lesson, didn't they?" Her grandfather smiled.

"I just hope they believe in Santa again. I hope the tree makes everyone believe."

"I think you could teach a lot of people some important lessons, Nicki. You've taught me more than I can count."

Nicki blushed. "Thank you."

The lights on the dashboard all lit up at once. "Two blocks away." SNOT's voice boomed through the speakers of the truck.

Grandpa reached over and put his hand on Nicki's shoulder. "This has been one of the best days of my life."

Nicki slid her hand over his. "Mine too, Grandpa."

"No matter what happens, we'll always have this, okay?"

Nicki tilted her head down and stared at the seat. "They're not going to let me see you again, are they?"

"Probably not." The words caught in his throat.

"It's not fair." Nicki leaned her head and rested it on top of their hands. "I only just got to meet you. I want to do this again. Every year."

"Ohh, Kiddo. I want that too. So so much." John sighed. "No matter what, I love you. And I'm so glad that you found out the truth about your gift and your family. A lot of people spend their whole lives looking for what makes them happy. You already found it." He smiled and blinked away a tear.

"I love you too, Grandpa."

The dashboard started to glow once more. "Turning down Main Street. This is it."

SNOT veered way out to the side and then made a hard left turn. His right front tire hopped up over the curb, just inches from the pole that held up the frost-covered traffic lights. When the tire fell back to the street Nicki and John bounced up and down on their seats.

They looked straight ahead to where they were going. Brutus growled.

Nicki gasped at the sight in front of her.

"No!"

CHAPTER FOURTEEN

THE MAN IN THE RED ROBE

Spectators lined the sides of the streets and glared or ran away with their children when the truck passed. The sun had just recently set and it was dark, though the road was illuminated by street lamps and lights from the buildings on all four sides. Nicki stared down the road.

Ahead of them sat a blockade formed by police cars, and at least twenty officers stood in front of them with their arms folded over their chests. Red and blue lights danced around the buildings.

Chakk-chackk-chak-chak-chak!

A beam of light lit up the hood of the truck. Nicki and John stared up at the sky. They both held a hand in front of their faces to block the blinding light. A helicopter hovered above, its propeller chopping through the frigid wind above the city.

"What do you want me to do?" SNOT asked over the speakers.

"Pull up in front of the police. I'll turn myself in. Once they remove the road block, you put the tree up for all the people."

SNOT and Nicki both spoke at the same time, "But—"

"We're not causing any trouble. The last thing we need is to have done all this for nothing. The tree is all that matters right now." He turned to look at Nicki. "Right, Kiddo?"

She nodded her head, even though tears streamed down her cheeks.

Nicki's heart beat faster and louder with every second that passed. When SNOT came to a halt in front of the officers, she unbuckled her seatbelt and leapt into her Grandfather's arms.

"Please don't go. Please. I'll talk to her. Don't go away. I don't want you to go." She knew her words probably made him feel worse, but she couldn't stop them. Nicki never asked anyone for anything, and she only wanted her grandfather. But, it seemed like there was no way she could have her wish.

"Your mother is protecting you. It's what good parents do. Look at me." He tilted her head up to face him. "Don't be mad at her, okay?"

Nicki nodded and he pulled her in so close that her cheek pressed against his chest and beard. Her tears soaked into his shirt and he smoothed her hair down the back of her head with his hand.

"It'll be okay. I promise. But we have to go so SNOT can get the job done."

"Step out of the vehicle with your hands behind your head." The words from the megaphone echoed through the streets and off the walls of the giant skyscrapers.

Brutus howled and Nicki covered her ears.

Grandpa released Nicki and two police officers ran around to his door with their guns drawn, probably because of Brutus and his bone-chilling growls.

"Go out that way." John nodded toward the driver's side door.

Nicki scooted reluctantly across the seat and opened it. She held her hands in the air and two other police officers grabbed her at once. The hackles on Brutus's neck raised, and John grabbed him around the neck. "It's okay, Boy. Go watch over her and make sure she's okay."

Nicki squealed and cried when they carried her away. Brutus followed but kept his distance from the officers. He stopped halfway and turned his head back to his master.

"Go on, Boy," John whispered, and waved his hand toward Nicki.

Brutus trotted in the snow after Nicki, but every few feet turned back and whimpered when his eyes met John's.

Two tears rolled down from the corners of John's eyes and dripped onto his cheeks before disappearing in his beard. He watched Nicki being carried away. Bent over one of their shoulders, she kicked and screamed and stretched her arms out, reaching back for him.

"Goodbye, Kiddo."

The passenger side door ripped open and John's back pounded the cold, wet pavement. It knocked all the air from his lungs and he gasped. Before he could catch his breath he was yanked to his feet and frigid, steel cuffs were snapped and tightened around his wrists.

The officers hauled him off toward one of the police cars. His legs wobbled like Jello, and he tried to stay on his feet through the slush. John peered over at Nicki.

Amanda hugged her frantically and checked her over to make sure she wasn't hurt. Nicki stared back at John with puffy red eyes while the police officers shoved him toward the back of a squad car. Brutus alternated between guarding Nicki and glancing back to John with high-pitched whimpers.

BOOM!

A bright flash of light.

The ground shook.

People shied away temporarily blinded, and held their hands up to their foreheads while their eyes adjusted.

Crunch. Crunch. Crunch.

Footsteps.

Loud ones.

With each step the ground rumbled as boots pounded against the ice and slush in the road.

Some of the police officers scattered and hid behind their cars.

Nicki stared down the road, her eyes still trying to adjust to the light.

A giant man, at least seven feet tall or more, appeared in the glow of the street lamps. As he neared, Nicki could see him more clearly and her heart very nearly stopped beating.

Every head and eye within the city block locked onto the man.

Ow-ow-owwwwwwlll!

Brutus belted out a bone-chilling howl that carried through the buildings, and multiplied as other dogs in the distance echoed his sentiments.

Nicki—and everyone else—glanced to Brutus and then quickly back to the imposing figure marching down the street.

High above the city the police chopper circled the towering skyscrapers, its blades whipping through the night air, keeping tabs on the events below. Its spotlight glowed bright and formed a shaky circle of light that remained glued to the giant man strolling down the street toward Nicki and the group of police officers. Packed sidewalks flanked the man on each side of the street and they stirred with each menacing step he took.

Nicki's breaths shallowed as the man closed the distance between them, and he grew larger in her field of vision with each crunch of his boots—large enough for her to make out details of his appearance.

His hair—long, platinum and slicked back—glimmered in the moonlight. It flowed down over his shoulders to the top of his back. A silvery beard like shiny, jagged icicles dripped from his chiseled, square jawline and chin. He could've easily been mistaken for a Norse God or a comic book character, only he appeared even more powerful and frightening. Nicki moved her shocked stare up to his eyes—a pair of solid black orbs—inside of which the Aurora Borealis glowed bright with greens and reds undulating in waves from side to side.

Nicki's stomach tightened like someone squeezed it in their palm.

The large man's eyebrows knit together, and he strode down the road in a smooth red robe that ran to his ankles. Nicki stared at the ornate cloak with silver stitching that swirled into words of an ancient Elven language and flowed into a gorgeous filigree.

People trembled at the sight of him and the police officers all held their hands over their gun holsters. Amanda's arms squeezed against Nicki, harder than she could ever remember being embraced.

The man walked up to Nicki and Amanda. He towered over everyone, and his shadow cast over the crowd.

Nicki held her breath and squished her eyes shut, afraid to look up at him.

Although she couldn't see with her eyes closed, she heard and felt him kneel down to the ground in front of her. She covered her eyes with her hands in case her curiosity got the best of her.

He reached out toward one of her hands and Amanda pressed Nicki closer to her.

"It's okay." The man's voice came out gruff, but surprisingly soft and warm. He reached out and took one of Nicki's hands and she allowed him to remove it from her face. Then he did the same with the other.

Nicki kept her eyes closed. She didn't want to shriek if she saw the giant up close.

"You can open your eyes, Nicoletta. I've waited a long time to see you again."

See me? Again?

Nicki slowly pried her eyes open and the man's appearance had changed. He wore a fuzzy red hat with a fluffy white ball of cotton on the end. His face was pudgy and round, his cheeks rosy. His beard was white and puffy like marshmallows. He smiled at Nicki. "Hi."

"Santa!" She flew out of her mother's hold and wrapped her arms around his wide shoulders. He hugged her back and looked up at Amanda and mouthed, 'it's okay' at her.

"Brutus, my boy! How have you been?" Santa scratched Brutus behind the ears.

Brutus barked twice at Santa.

"Oh, you've been good this year, have you?"

Brutus barked once this time.

Santa reached into a pocket and widened his eyes at Nicki. When he pulled his hand out and opened it a Milk-Bone sat in his palm, and he grinned at her. "Watch this, we used to do it all the time."

Brutus tried to sit still, but Nicki noticed his tail swooshing the snow back and forth.

Santa tossed the treat in the air and Brutus caught it with a loud crunch, and chomped it down.

Amanda cupped a hand over her mouth

and stared in disbelief.

Santa belted out a hearty laugh, and then turned back to Nicki.

"But, but, you looked—I mean I saw—" Nicki couldn't form a sentence. Too many thoughts rushed through her head.

"You saw me the way the others did at first."

"I-I don't understand."

"Well, it's easy really. People see me with their heart and not their eyes. Many people around here have forgotten Christmas, have forgotten what it means to believe. They became afraid when I showed up. People fear what they don't understand."

"So you looked scary because they were scared?"

Santa glanced up to Amanda who remained pale and visibly shaken. "You have a very smart little girl here."

Amanda nodded up and down quickly.

Santa glanced over to John and the police officer that held him outside of the squad car door. "Jimmy Standwick, release him or you can kiss that NFL Sunday Package goodbye." Santa waggled his bushy eyebrows at Nicki.

She giggled and smiled.

The officer's eyes grew wide and he looked over at what appeared to be his boss, another man in uniform. The other man nodded, and Jimmy uncuffed Grandpa.

"Hey John. It's good to see family," said Santa.

Amanda gasped. Nicki took a step over and hugged her. "You didn't know that we're related to Santa Claus?"

Amanda gawked, still unable to speak. Her teeth chattered together as she shook her head back and forth, staring at Santa Claus.

Santa took a step toward Amanda, his waist big and round and he stood only an inch or two taller than her. He held his white, glove-covered hands up and placed them on her cheeks. "Nicholas loved you very much." He paused and sighed. "Very, very much, Amanda."

Amanda's eyes began to mist and her shoulders trembled.

"He walked away from the family business when he followed you off to college. He didn't know how you'd react to the news, and he couldn't risk losing you because of it."

"H-he was afraid I wouldn't believe him?"

"Oh, no. No, Child." Santa slid one hand to Amanda's shoulder. "He just wanted a normal life for you and him. That's all."

John sauntered over toward them. "I-I didn't know that's why he left."

Santa turned to him. "Ohh yes. He loved driving the truck. But he loved Amanda even more. He knew he couldn't talk her into staying, and wouldn't last a day without being near her."

Santa Claus bent down so that he was eye level with Nicki. "And he loved you, sweet Nicoletta. He loved you so much."

Nicki's whole body warmed, despite the chill wind that whipped between the buildings and across her ears.

"I'm very sorry, Amanda." John took off his

wool cap and held it down at his waist with both hands. "I never knew how much my son loved you. I thought it was a high school crush. I didn't understand him as much as I thought I did. And I never knew about this amazing young girl until she showed up at my house yesterday." He nodded to Nicki. "I'm sorry that we made you worry, but I would never put her in harm's way." John let out a long sigh. "What happened, the night of Nicholas's accident. He told you he got called into work, but he was driving the truck for me to go get the tree. I'd called for Santa to get help. I was sick. So sick I couldn't walk." John's eyes closed and he fought back a sob. His lip quivered when he spoke. "B-but he'd b-been away too long—grown older. The magic he came from had faded, and when h-h-he—" He sniffled and tears streamed from John's eyes, and he choked on his words. "I-It's a long story, b-but—"

Amanda reached out and took one of his hands. "But we have plenty of time to tell it later. Don't we?"

John sniffled once more. "Y-yeah, I suppose we do. So does this mean—"

Amanda smiled through tears of her own. "Isn't forgiveness part of Christmas?" She turned to Santa. "That's right, isn't it?"

Santa Claus grinned. "Indeed. Indeed it is, Amanda."

Amanda stepped toward John and nearly tackled him with a hug, taking him by surprise. His eyes widened and then closed. He pulled her in closer and they both failed to fight back tears of happiness.

"I'm sorry too. I forgot I wasn't the only one who lost him when it happened. But we're here now." She leaned back and stared into her father-in-law's eyes tucked behind his snowy white beard. "And we're not going anywhere."

John embraced her once more in his arms and closed his eyes.

Everybody in the crowd—including the police officers—cheered and clapped. Nicki smiled up at her grandfather. His eyes opened a little to peek at her and he gave her a thumbs up. She did the same right back at him. Brutus barked a few times and then panted with his long pink tongue hanging from his mouth.

"Hey Pal, you gonna move that thing so I can put on a show here or what? The talent has arrived." SNOT's windshield wipers waggled up and down.

The officer's mouth dropped open and he tugged on the uniform sleeve of the officer next to him. "D-did y-you see that? That tr-tr-truck just talked to me."

"Huh? Man are you crazy, or what?"

"Oh, I'm crazy? We got Santa Claus out here in the street and you're acting like I'm crazy. Sheesh."

"Hey, guys. I ain't got all day here." SNOT's headlights widened at them.

"Holy mother—" The second officer's jaw dropped to the ground.

"Told you I wasn't crazy."

They both scurried to move the police cars.

"Okay, back it up, people. Move on out and let the truck through." Both officers waved people back and jumped in their cars.

Nicki wrapped her arms around the waists of Amanda and John. They both reached down and hugged her back.

"I want to know everything. I see so much of him in you and her." Amanda held her palm to Nicki's cheek.

"I'll tell you whatever you want to know. I want to know all about you guys too," said John.

"Hey, Girlie Face! Check this out!" SNOT hollered. He swung the mechanical arms of the truck up into the air. "You want to help me pump up the crowd for this, or what?"

Brutus trotted over to Santa and licked his boots.

John shook his head at SNOT. "He's always had to pretend he was a normal truck before. I guess this is a new era."

"Mommy, can I go over there with SNOT?"

"Why on earth do you call him snot?"

Nicki and her grandfather giggled.

"They think they're funny. That Claus family tree grew a bunch of jokesters on it, I swear. Pffft!"

Amanda giggled with Nicki. Nicki couldn't remember the last time her mom giggled like that.

"Sure, go on. But wear your seatbelt and be careful!" Amanda wagged a finger at Nicki, but she was already halfway to the truck. "You hurt her, and your name will be the least of your concerns!" The wagging finger turned to SNOT.

SNOT cowered. "Yes, ma'am."

Nicki came trotting up to him. "She doesn't mess around. I'd do what she says."

"Oh, I plan to."

Amanda shook her head at John. "She already loved trucks. Now she has one that talks."

"She sure does." John stared at her and SNOT joking with each other. "I'll never get him back now."

John and Amanda looked at each other and smiled.

"Hey Nicki, check this out. Pull my tire." SNOT hiked the driver's side wheel up to her.

Nicki strained and groaned, tugging on it with both arms.

SNOT's headlights squeezed shut and the truck started to shake like he was bearing down.

BRRRRRRTTTTT!

A puff of smoke blew out of one of the exhaust pipes sprouting up out of the hood.

Nicki clutched her ribs and she and SNOT died laughing.

"I just—" John looked away from Amanda and shook his head, though he still smiled.

Amanda's cheeks puffed out, like she was holding back a laugh. "They're two of a kind. Aren't they?"

"Yep."

"All right, Nicki. Hop in and let's show these people what Christmas is all about." SNOT's driver's side door swung open. "I need a jolt of that cheer you got. Then we're gonna rock this crowd."

"Sounds like a plan!" Nicki climbed up into the truck and then held the seatbelt up so Amanda could see it through the window.

John gave her another thumbs up.

Once Nicki was secure, she gripped the wheel and SNOT belted out a, "Wooo!" The dashboard lit up. "Let's get this show on the road. I mean, we're on the road already, but you know what I mean, Girlie Face!"

Nicki giggled.

SNOT unhooked the trailer from the truck and drove out into the middle of the street. His headlights closed and he struck a pose suggesting he was about to put on some kind of routine.

The crowd of people along the street cheered.

"Gotta be kidding me." John covered his face with his hand and shook his head.

The edge of SNOT's grill moved like he was whispering out the side of his mouth. It was a low mutter.

"Christ-mas Tree. Christ-mas Tree." He attempted to start a chant.

It worked. People started to chant the word up and down the road. SNOT stayed in his pose, waiting for it to grow louder and louder.

Soon, the words boomed through the city and echoed up the buildings into the sky. One by one the street lamps went out and the lights of the buildings flickered and then shut off.

It was pitch black.

Carol of the Bells started to play over SNOT's speakers, at a low volume at first but slowly growing louder. White beams of light shot from the truck and formed snowflakes on the walls and buildings. They danced around to the sounds of the stringed instruments.

People held their children and hugged them tight, pointing at the lights while the little ones gazed. Christmas lights and a talking truck seemed to hold their attention.

"Who's ready for a Christmas Tree?" SNOT shouted.

Cheers rang out and the violins and cellos turned to electric guitars that exploded through the speakers. The lights grew brighter and sped up on the walls. Tiny LED lights lit up on SNOT and he looked like a truck covered in sparkly white diamonds. The trailer glowed the same. The bass from the music shook the ground and Nicki covered her ears while she sat inside and watched it all take place from the driver's seat of the truck.

"I can't hear you! Show me your Christmas spirit!"

The two arms popped out from the side of the truck. They too were covered in lights, and SNOT waved them up and down like a football player on the field riling up the crowd.

Claps, cheers, whistles, whoops, and hollers—all of the sounds turned into a giant roar that boomed through the city.

SNOT revved the engine and started whipping in a circle, doing a donut in the street to the cheers of the crowd. The lights on the walls formed different shapes, changing from snowflakes, to angels, to a truck, to a tree, and then to Santa Claus and gift boxes.

Nicki clutched the seat and squealed a happy squeal as they spun in a circle. SNOT came to a stop and Nicki looked out into the sky, along with the rest of the crowd who craned their necks up to see what the other sound was.

The Viking sleigh shot up into the night sky, and Santa's platinum, sleek hair blew in the wind. The ground rumbled and shook beneath the feet of the crowd as they craned their heads up toward the night sky and searched for the seemingly mythical figure they'd all just witnessed with their own eyes. The reindeer were large and imposing, so much so that every mouth fell open when the silhouettes of their lightning bolt antlers and muscular Clydesdale-like bodies passed in front of the full moon.

"Woww!" Nicki gasped, drawing out the word.

The sleigh, Santa, and the reindeer suddenly morphed in the middle of the sky into the classic Santa figure that they all knew and loved as children. Their gallops no longer shook the ground, and bells jingled when their legs kicked against the air. Santa sat in the middle of the sleigh—round and portly—just like described in all the stories Nicki read and movies she watched.

Nicki smiled and peered around at the crowd. They all stared up in reverie, childish grins plastered to their faces, their hearts saturated with joy, and they saw the jolly Santa.

The city—the same city that for the last eight years starved itself of the Christmas spirit—glowed bright with cheer.

"Ho, ho, ho." The voice faded along with the sleigh into the night.

"That guy is always stealing my thunder," SNOT muttered.

"It's okay, SNOT." Nicki patted the steering wheel.

The dash glowed bright once more. "No, I mean literally. Did you hear those reindeer?"

Nicki laughed. "Well they're counting on *us* now. Let's give the people a show!"

"Now you're talkin', Kid."

SNOT blasted the music and the cheers rang out even louder than before, a new energy circulating through the streets. "You folks ready for a Christmas tree?"

Whoops and hollers of, "YES!" filled the air.

SNOT held up a tire to one of his side mirrors, like he was cupping a hand to his ear. "I can't hear youuu!"

The cheers grew louder.

He did the same to the other side of the road, and the crowd's shouts grew deafening.

"Ladies and gentlemen, I present to you this year's Christmas tree!"

The song *O' Christmas Tree* blared through the speakers and the crowd fell silent.

All of the lights focused onto the tree, and the crane slowly rose from the trailer. SNOT drove over and hooked himself back up to it and then pulled it down in front of the lot.

Every eye in the street focused on the tree and the crane.

Snap.

Snap.

Snap.

The restraints unlatched one at a time down the trailer, and the branches of the tree spilled over the side.

The hook lowered from the crane and attached itself around the top of the tree.

"Oooh." Every person, from the youngest to the oldest, gasped when the crane lifted the tree upright in the trailer bed.

The dashboard lit up and SNOT spoke only to Nicki. "Should we decorate this thing for them?"

"Oh yes, please." Nicki still gazed at the beauty of the tree as she hung her head out of the window to see it behind them.

SNOT's arms moved out slowly, still covered in sparkling lights that outlined the shape. The crane rotated the tree in a slow circle as the arms held up the lights. The arms moved down slowly, wrapping the lights perfectly around the tree. Next was red and gold garland, and then the hands on the ends of SNOT's arms hung large red and gold ornaments all over it.

Once finished, the crane slowly swung the big tree over to the empty area where the Christmas tree once stood each year. The music continued to play soft piano notes. SNOT's arms tied steel cables to the middle of the tree while the crane kept it steady. Another arm moved slowly toward the tree, the hum of its motor barely heard over the music.

With one big and mighty swing, it drove a steel stake with the support cable attached into the ground. The arm moved and repeated this until the tree was held up by four support stakes.

"You ready for the finale?" SNOT asked Nicki.

She stared at the tree through the passenger side window. It looked even taller than it did in the wild, only now it had lights and ornaments and garland wrapped around it. It glowed even brighter from the reflections off the glass of the buildings.

"Uh huh." She nodded, still halfway in a trance.

The crane unhooked from the tree and swung back over to the truck.

Slowly rising up in the truck bed was a giant crystal star, handcrafted by the elves far before the Christmas truck was ever built.

Nicki couldn't see it yet, but she heard the "oohs" and "aahs" from the people standing on the sidewalks.

John put his arm around Amanda as they watched the star float up to the top of the tree. Brutus howled once more and Amanda patted him on the head. When the star came to rest and lit up high above the crowd, the music changed to *We Wish You a Merry Christmas* and people up and down the sidewalk began to sing along. There were cheers and shouts, whooping and hollering. The Christmas spirit had returned to the city stronger than ever. And it all happened because Nicki Noel believed that she could drive a curious-looking Christmas truck.

Nicki looked up at the star high in the night sky, atop the tree, and she smiled. "This is for you, Dad."

Epilogue

LIGHTS GLEAMED THROUGH the windows of John's house up on the mountainside. It was Christmas Eve and for the first time in many, many years, laughter sounded from inside of his home. Around a large oak table that filled most of the dining room, Nicki, Amanda, John, Grant, and Liz smiled and laughed and told Christmas stories both new and old.

John walked in from the kitchen carrying a huge pot of turkey and noodles, and bowls and serving platters full of other heavenly-smelling side dishes were arranged neatly out in front of Nicki's eyes. Her mouth practically watered at the sight and smells of all the delicious food.

"Can we really move up here, Mom?" Nicki bounced in her chair.

"I'm working on it." Amanda smiled at John, then glanced down at Nicki. "But I really, really hope so!"

Nicki thought about how much Christmas had changed for her that year. The city was decorated with wreaths and big red bows and greenery and Christmas lights. Earlier in the day she'd seen the man in the Santa Claus suit ringing his bell and smiling huge while he collected spare change from people to help buy toys for kids. Nicki had walked over and handed him her dollar she'd received for doing all her chores at home without being asked.

"*Merry Christmas!*" he'd shouted at anyone that passed, whether they gave money or not. Nicki couldn't have been happier than she was at that very moment, at least she thought.

After their meal, John, Grant, Nicki, and Brutus fanned out in a half-circle around the fireplace. Stockings hung down from the mantle, and they'd put a Christmas tree up in the corner of the living room. In the middle of the tree hung the ornament that Amanda had promised Nicki—an 18-wheeler and not a pick-up truck. Nicki had her feet propped up on the bricks like usual, to keep her toes warm and toasty. She looked around at the Christmas decorations, John's smiling face, and the rest of the people she loved. She scrubbed Brutus behind his ears and giggled at the red bow she'd attached to his collar. "You're my Christmas present," she whispered in his ear. His cold, wet nose pressed against her cheek and he licked her face, eliciting even more giggles from her.

Amanda and Liz chatted in the kitchen and made hot chocolate for everyone. Not the powdered kind that John had made when he first met Nicki, but the kind with milk and bars of chocolate melted into a pot on the stove with marshmallows. Nicki wasn't sure where she was going to put hers, because her stomach was so packed with turkey and noodles and mashed potatoes and green beans and milk.

They all enjoyed the hot cocoa and told more stories of Christmas time and Nicki's favorite—stories about Nicholas. Some were funny and some were serious, but Nicki loved all of them the same, and she felt like she knew her father even better each time she heard one.

Grant and Liz finally left to head back down the mountain to their house, but they promised Nicki they'd come back in the morning to open presents.

After Nicki dressed in her pajamas and said her prayers, she climbed up into her father's old bed and snuggled under the covers. She lifted her head from the soft pillow and peered around at the pictures of Nicholas that hung on the walls. It was her favorite room in the whole world. She imagined her father as a boy on Christmas Eve, lying down in the same bed and in the same spot as her. His stomach was probably full of food and tingled with anticipation, just like Nicki's at that very moment. She shut her eyes for a brief second and could feel her dad's arms wrapped around her and heard his voice in her ear. "I'm so proud of you, Nicki."

"So which book do you want to read, Kiddo?"

Nicki's eyes popped open and she turned her head to the door. John leaned against the frame with a comforting smile on his face.

Amanda walked in behind John and they both climbed into bed with her.

Nicki stared playfully at her grandfather. "I think you already know."

"Yes." John grinned. "I believe I do." He reached over to the bookshelf for *Twas the Night Before Christmas* and handed it to Nicki.

"Mom look!" She held up the book to Amanda. "Do you want to see Dad's handwriting when he was a little boy?"

Nicki flipped the book open to the page before her mother could even answer.

"Ooh, Nicki. Would you look at that?" Amanda took the book from Nicki and ran her finger along the letters before hugging it to her chest. "You know—" Amanda smiled at John. "His handwriting really never got much better than this."

They all chuckled.

"All right, Kiddo. You ready?" asked John.

Nicki shook her head, lying between the two people she loved most in the world. "Not yet."

Grandpa's eyebrows raised and he scratched his beard. "What are you waiting for?"

"Brutus!" Nicki called.

John chuckled.

Brutus's large paws thundered up the wooden stairs and the bed shook when he leapt up on the end of it. Nicki glanced to John in the corner of her eye.

He stared back at her like she had sprouted a second head.

Nicki shrugged. "What? I need my foot warmer." She sat up and leaned down to scratch Brutus on the top of his head, his favorite place to be scratched. He panted from all the running and leaping, but managed to lick one of her fingers before she pulled her hand back.

"Okay, Kiddo. You've got this down now. Right?"

"Yep!"

Nicki read the first half of the story without stuttering one single word. She paused in the middle of a sentence and stretched her arms way up over her head, as far as she could reach and yawned wide. "I ate too much, Grandpa. It's making me sleepy. Can you or Mom finish for me?"

Amanda rubbed Nicki's back and smiled at John. "You did very good, Sweetie."

"Thank you, Mommy." Nicki curled up next to her mother and propped her head on her stomach.

John and Amanda took turns reading pages of the story. Nicki faded a little more with each word. Her long eyelashes fluttered and her eyelids grew heavier with each second that passed. When John finished the last page, he glanced over and Nicki was sound asleep on her mom.

He shut the book and placed it back on the shelf.

When he turned back to the girls his heart grew warm and happy. Amanda had fallen asleep with her head up against the bed rest and Nicki cradled in her arms.

John stood from the bed and pulled the covers up to their necks. He kissed his hand and put it on each one of their heads. "Sleep well, girls."

He walked from the room full of Christmas joy.

❄ ❄ ❄

Nikki jolted up from her sleep. It was all too familiar, like she was reliving the night Giftavius showed up to help with SNOT. Pictures rattled against the walls like there was an earthquake, exactly the same as they had before.

"Ho ho ho." The words fell into Nicki's ears from far away in the distance, but the whooshing wind sped up outside of her window.

"Whoa fellas!"

A large shadow blew past her window and rattled the pane of glass. Nicki heard hooves slam into the ground and gallop to a halt. She reached over and shook her mother but Amanda was far away, deep in a dream somewhere, and she wouldn't wake up.

Nicki hopped down from the bed and skipped through the hallway. She ran down the stairs and threw on her cap, shoes, and her father's jacket.

Bolting through the door, she flew into the front yard and turned to the sleigh. Some of the snow from the blizzard had melted away, but enough remained to still cover the ground.

She rubbed her eyes to make sure she was awake and her blurred vision came into focus.

There was Santa—the happy, round jolly version of him—standing casually and chit-chatting with SNOT.

"Oh, there you are!" He held out his arms.

Nicki rubbed her eyes once more and smiled a toothy grin. "Did you make it? To all the kids' houses?"

Santa Claus strode toward her, his cheeks rosy and his smile growing by the second. His black boots crunched the snow beneath them. "Oh yes, Nicoletta. I made it to each and every house in record time, seeing as I had both trees up this year." Once he was in front of her, he extended his index finger and booped her on the nose.

Nicki's cheeks filled with pink and she clapped and squealed.

Santa dropped to a knee so that he was at eye level with her. "And I couldn't have done it without you."

"Hey!" SNOT hollered from a little ways away.

"Oh, my apologies. And you, SNOT."

"Thanks, Santa!" SNOT's voice sounded like an excited little boy who yearned for Santa's approval.

"You're my last stop before the North Pole. I'm so very glad that you woke up to come see me."

"I wouldn't have missed this for the world."

"Well, well. You're too kind to this jolly old man." Santa rose to his feet and rubbed his round belly. "I have a very, very important question for you, Nicoletta."

Nicki twiddled her thumbs. "What is it, Santa?"

"Well—" He made a show of scratching his beard and looked up toward the night sky before glancing back down at her. "I need to know what *you* want for Christmas. You never told me. I know because I've checked off every name on the nice list, except for one." He tapped her lightly on the nose with his index finger once more. "Yours."

Nicki thought long and hard and stared up at the bright twinkling stars and big yellow moon. After a few moments, she looked back at Santa Claus. "I know you have to get back to the North Pole, Santa. So if it's too much trouble, then it's okay." She looked down at the ground.

Santa softly reached under her chin and tilted her face back to his rosy red cheeks and large, round eyes. "Don't be afraid to ask for what you want, Nicoletta. You've already done more for Christmas than anyone could ever imagine. You're never too much trouble for me."

Nicki's smile returned to her face. "Can you visit the two boys from my class? The ones who told me that girls can't drive trucks and that you aren't real? And can you take them some extra toys, so that they'll keep believing in you?"

Santa's thick white bushy eyebrows rose on

his forehead. "Is that what you want most of all?"

"Yes, Sir. I want them to believe in you as much as I do."

Santa knelt down to Nicki once more. He reached out with a white, glove-covered hand and lightly rubbed up and down on the back of Nicki's arm. "Nicoletta, you have a light inside of you that will never burn out. I truly mean that."

Nicki blushed. "Thank you, Santa."

"Ooh, Child, you are so very welcome. And I promise to take care of your request before I return home, okay?"

Nicki chewed on her bottom lip to contain her joy and then smiled at Santa Claus. "Okay."

"Now run off to bed and go back to sleep. I'll see you again soon." He leaned over and gave her a quick peck on the forehead. "Merry Christmas."

"Merry Christmas, Santa."

Nicki heard Brutus whining from behind the front door. She turned around to the door and when she looked back, Santa and the sleigh were gone.

How did he disappear like that? Nicki thought.

She stood for a quick second, and scanned the night sky but couldn't see him in the dark. "Goodnight, Santa," she whispered.

Somewhere—so far off in the distance that Nicki couldn't tell which direction it came from—she heard Santa's voice.

"Ho ho ho. Merry Christmas to all, and to all a good night."

Nicki walked back to her room and climbed into bed with Brutus following closely behind. She stared at her mother who still slept peacefully with her arms wrapped tight around a pillow, and her blanket scrunched up down at her waist.

"Goodnight, Mommy. I love you."

Nicki leaned over and kissed her mother on the cheek, then pulled the covers back up to her neck. Amanda nuzzled into the pillow and talked in her sleep.

"Nicholas, did you know we're related to Santa Claus?" Amanda's mouth curled into a sheepish grin.

It made Nicki giggle and she covered her mouth. She didn't want to wake her mom while she dreamt about Nicholas.

Nicki slid under the covers and wrapped an arm around her mom, then she closed her eyes and fell back asleep.

❄ ❄ ❄

The next morning a bright flash of sunlight from the window made its way to the bed. Nicki's eyes sprang open.

It's Christmas morning!

She couldn't remember if she had dreamt about Santa or not. Brutus stirred awake at her feet, and then hopped lazily off the bed. He leaned out and stretched his front legs, and then followed suit with the back ones.

Nicki sniffed the air, but didn't smell any snow coming. She rubbed her knuckles in her eyes, and was still trying to fully wake up. What found her nose though, was her second favorite smell in the whole world—bacon. She reached over for her mom but Amanda wasn't in the bed. It took Nicki a few more seconds to get her wits about her, and then she remembered again why she'd just gotten so excited. She froze stiff.

It's Christmas morning!

She didn't skip to the stairs on that Christmas morning. Nicki Noel sprinted across the carpet and down the stairs.

She heard Grant and Liz laughing and talking with John and Amanda. Tingles of anticipation rippled through Nicki's stomach, and she couldn't get to the living room fast enough.

She slid around the corner on her socks where the stairs ended. It was a lot like SNOT fishtailing around the curvy roads in the snow.

Nicki righted herself after nearly colliding with the wall and stared straight ahead. Christmas gifts spilled out from under the tree. They were all different shapes and sizes and were covered with bows and wrapping paper.

"Merry Christmas, Sweetie." Amanda stood in front of the stove flipping bacon in a pan. "You want some breakfast?"

"No time!" She ran over in front of the tree and gawked. "Look at all of them, Mommy!"

Amanda walked toward the living room.

"What is it? Did Santa come?" Amanda winked playfully at John and he grinned.

"Yeah."

Amanda stared at Nicki with a puzzled look. "Well don't sound too excited about it."

"Why would I get excited now?" Nicki shrugged. "I talked to him for like five minutes out in the yard last night."

Amanda turned to John and he held his hands up playfully in defense. "I didn't know. Take that one up with the big guy."

Amanda tried to hide a smile and look serious. "This family, I swear." She shook her head and turned back to Nicki. "Well, someone must have been a really good girl for Santa to have come."

"I was, Mommy. I promise."

Liz and Grant smiled and waved hello to Nicki.

Amanda walked over and sat down on the couch. John hunkered down in the recliner.

"Which one do you want to open first?" Amanda asked.

Nicki held her index finger to her lips and looked over all of them. Front to back, side to side, up and down—she peered at them from every angle possible.

There was one smaller gift in front of them all, right in the center. It was a thin square shape, and had a special silvery wrapping paper with white snowflakes all over it. There was a card attached that said "Nicoletta" in flowery handwriting.

Amidst all the large boxes and ornately wrapped gifts, that one present seemed to call to her. She picked it up and squeezed it tight to her chest with a cheery smile. "This one."

"Well come over here and open it." Amanda scooched over on the couch.

Nicki walked over and sat down next to her mother, then ran her fingers along the wrapping paper and traced the handwriting on the card.

Her stomach fluttered when she started to peel the layers covering the gift. It crinkled and crackled in her fingers. She sat the card down on her thigh once she had one end of the gift opened and carefully slid it out from the silver paper.

Once she wrestled it free, Nicki couldn't stop her eyes from watering. Her vision blurred from all the tears and she clapped a hand over her mouth. Nicki tried to blink them from her eyes, but the more she tried to resist the more overwhelmed she became. She clutched her present to her chest. Her tears turned to sobs and she lunged into her mother's arms and buried her face in her sweater.

"What is it, sweetie? Don't cry." Amanda hugged her trembling daughter tight and kissed her head over and over. "What is it?"

Nicki couldn't stop shaking against her mother, but her sobs and tears weren't from sadness. They were from the exact opposite, in fact.

Nicki slowly held her gift up for Amanda to see.

It was a picture of Santa Claus. He cradled

an infant Nicki in a hospital room, and her father, Nicholas, stood next to him with one hand on his shoulder. Nick's other hand was caressing Nicki's cheek, and he was staring at her like she was the most beautiful thing he'd ever seen.

"Oh my goodness." Amanda gasped and squeezed her daughter harder.

Nicki had wished so many times that she could have just one picture with her dad. She'd always wanted one more than anything—more than any truck or toy, or even more than she'd wanted to drive SNOT up the mountain to get the Christmas tree—but she'd never told anybody, because she didn't think any existed.

Nicki looked once more at the picture. She still couldn't contain the tears and handed it to Amanda, before nuzzling back into her sweater. Amanda held the picture up for all of the others to see.

"Ohh," said John, Grant, and Liz at the same time. Each of them smiled at Nicki and wiped the corners of their eyes—even Grant.

Nicki sniffled and looked up at her mom. She barely choked out her words. "I-It's a p-p-picture of m-m-me and m-m-my D-d-daddy." By the time she got to the word 'daddy' her lip was quivering, and she broke into another fit of tears.

Amanda clutched Nicki's head in her palms and whispered, "I know, Sweetie. I saw it. It's a beautiful picture." She rubbed her hand up and down Nicki's back. "How many kids can say they're related to Santa Claus and that he held them as a baby?" She turned to John. "How did he find us in the hospital that day? I didn't think anyone knew where we were. They must have taken me away for something and Nicholas snuck him in." She chuckled at the thought of Santa being smuggled into the hospital and shook her head. "Totally something he would've done."

"Yep," said all three of them at the same time again.

"He's Santa Claus. He always knows," said John.

Nicki had finally gotten her emotions under control and stared around at everyone. "Sorry, I just got so—I don't know if I want to open any more presents." Nicki grinned and gazed back at the picture.

Everyone laughed.

Nicki scooped up the card that had fallen down to the floor. Only Santa Claus and Giftavius had ever called her Nicoletta, the name written on the card. She opened it slowly and read the words inside. The handwriting was just slightly neater than the words in the *Twas the Night Before Christmas* book upstairs.

Nicoletta,

You can do anything and be anything that you want, as long as you always believe. You and your mother will forever be my Christmas miracle. I'll always be with you.

Love,

Dad

Note From the Author

Thank you for reading Nicki Noel and the Curious Christmas Truck. Writing this book has been one of the most incredible and rewarding experiences of my career thus far. There were many reasons for writing this book.

I have a four-year-old son (at the time of publication) and the books I write under other various pen names are not appropriate for children. At four-years-old, my son will soon begin asking questions about what his dad does for a living. It's inevitable, the stage when children become curious about their parents—what they do, who they are.

I didn't want to answer the question of what I do with, "I make up stories for a living, Son. But you're too young to read them." I wanted to be able to show him with a story. My job is amazing and I wanted to be able to share it with him on an intimate level.

So I decided to write a book for him. A book tailored to him that could teach him lessons and create conversations that I wanted to have with him. He's enamored with trucks and tractors and trains—any big machines really.

He has the toys and watches the television shows. He builds and creates and loves to know how these machines work. He also loves Christmas and Santa Claus (or Sin Caus, as he calls him).

I also wanted to write a book that he'd enjoy reading for years, so I decided to write a chapter book. Reading is very important, and I wanted a book that would challenge him up through his teen years, and one that he could still read up through adulthood. A book that was his, that he could say, "My dad wrote this for me."

The mind of a child is a precious, beautiful, and fleeting thing. A child's innocence is one of the most amazing miracles on the planet. His mother and I would like to keep that intact for as long as possible, and I wanted this story to reflect that and for it to be one of the main themes of the book, along with the importance of women's equality, giving, change, redemption, and belief in one's self.

It was a challenge for sure. I'd never written a book for this age group. The experience was eye opening. But, I wouldn't change it for the world. I absolutely loved writing it and will probably write more in this genre. I love writing different things and growing as an author, adding more tools to my repertoire. I hope that children and adults got as much out of reading this story as I did writing it. Thank you so much for spending some of your time with my words.

Acknowledgements

First and foremost, I'd like to thank my wife, who put up with me scrambling to get this story done before Christmas this year. For reading and supporting the book, and for making notes and all her suggestions. I couldn't have written this without your encouragement, love, and support. I love you, babe!

I'd like to thank my copy editors, Stacey and Trina at Spellbound, for making sure it was typo free and readable. They are amazing and always prompt and professional.

Thank you to Lisa Reads at BTP designs for creating a cover that brings this story to life! It's beautiful, as are all your covers, and I can't express my gratitude enough.

Thank you to my beta readers, Maggie Jane Shuler, Little, and Middle. This book wouldn't have been the same without you. The kind words and encouragement coupled with the notes were invaluable. Thank you Crystal Jimenez, and her children Kira and JJ for all of their feedback. Thank you Marlena Salinas my buddy reader. You always give me fantastic feedback and criticism. To all of my beta readers, your kind words and help mean the world to me and I can't thank you enough for them. I'm so ecstatic that you were able to bond with me over my words and be a part of this story that I'm incredibly proud of.

Thank you to all of my fans and book bloggers who read and reviewed this "different" creation of mine. I couldn't do this without any of you. You all give me the special gift of making up stories for a living, but my job as a father is the ultimate dream job and this project specifically embraced that. The fact that you are always willing to accept and support the quirky projects I come up with just further tells me what great friends you truly are. So thank you, so very much! Words can't express my gratitude.

Thank you to all of my author colleagues who are always there to dish out advice and support, especially when I freak out and think my stories are crap (which is often). You're always a fantastic shoulder to lean on, and I'm always here to return the favor when you need it. I couldn't ask for a better group of work friends.

Lastly, but most importantly, thank you to my son, the Boy. You inspire me every single day and never cease to bring a smile to my face. You are my greatest accomplishment, simply because you exist. I love you more than life itself, and I always will for the rest of your life and beyond. My love for you has no requirements. No matter what you do and no matter what life throws our way, it will always be there and it will always shine as bright as it did the first day I laid eyes on your precious face and you squeezed your tiny fingers around mine. Nothing you can do will ever change that. Dah ee loves you.

Made in the USA
Middletown, DE
01 December 2017